NO PROMISES

BRENDA BARRETT

"**I** didn't remember that your brothers had a restaurant here," Chex said. "It never clicked in my mind when I stopped here that this place was owned by your family. I guess I wasn't thinking, but it's obvious now, the silver in Silver Spoon. "

"Yup," Garnet nodded. "Usually, you are sharper than that."

Chex grimaced. "I am out of sorts today, and to be fair, there are so many changes in this place. I can vaguely recall this spot being a cattle pasture."

"Yes," Garnet said, "things change."

"Like the fact that you have a kid," Chex said, abruptly changing the topic from Crimson Hill and its changes.

"I have a kid," Garnet repeated.

"Why does he look like my brother?" Chex asked, leaning forward.

"Which one of your brothers?" Garnet smirked.

"Phillip," Chex said. "Phillip looks like Dad. Is he Phillip's kid?"

Garnet shook her head. "Guess again."

ALSO BY BRENDA BARRETT

FULL CIRCLE
NEW BEGINNINGS
THE PREACHER AND THE PROSTITUTE
AFTER THE END
THE EMPTY HAMMOCK
THE PULL OF FREEDOM
REBOUND SERIES
THREE RIVERS SERIES
NEW SONG SERIES
BANCROFT SERIES
MAGNOLIA SISTERS SERIES
SCARLETT SERIES
WILEY BROTHERS SERIES
PRYCE SISTERS SERIES
THE JACKSONS SERIES

ABOUT THE AUTHOR

Brenda Barrett is an award-winning and bestselling author who has a passion for writing real Jamaican romances.

When she's not weaving words that transport readers to exotic locales, you can find her nurturing her green thumb in the garden or doting on her beloved cats.

With an infectious zest for life, this author brings a unique perspective to her writing that is both relatable and thought-provoking.

Don't be surprised if you find yourself lost in the pages of her latest work, as she seamlessly blends romance with some drama, mystery, and suspense, or even sci-fi, leaving readers wanting more.

You can connect with Brenda online at:
Brenalbar.com
Twitter.com/AuthorWriterBB
Facebook.com/AuthorBrendaBarrett

Chapter One

Why did he let his therapist convince him to come to Crimson Hills? Chex thought darkly as he sat in the back of the town car on the way to his father's funeral. He didn't need closure; he wasn't grieving. He felt nothing. He had escaped the place when he was sixteen and had legally changed his name from Knight to Hastings when he was eighteen. Since he had left twenty years ago, he had not been back to Knightsbridge, their seventy-acre farm in the hills.

"Why did you leave up here in the first place?" Dana asked chirpily. "It's gorgeous! I could see myself doing a vacation up here. Do you know what this place reminds me of? Taormina in Sicily. It's the rolling hills and the sea in the distance."

Chex sighed; Dana had insisted on going with him instead of traveling with the bus that the Hastings family had hired to transport the clan to support his mother. Dana was one of the Hastings cousins. His grandfather, Eustace, had one child, Laurel, Chex's mom, but Eustace's siblings had dozens of children, and Dana was one of them. Her home base was in New York, but she was always traveling. He had casually mentioned to her that Maurice had died, and Dana had booked a flight to attend the funeral. She was staying at the Hastings mansion in the guest house. He had taken her partying the night before, mostly so that he didn't have to talk about his father's passing.

He didn't know why people thought he would be feeling some sort of remorse when Maurice died. He would have preferred not to even acknowledge it. His father had been dead and buried in his head for years now. He was itching to tell Danger to turn the car around and head back to Kingston. Attending this funeral would be a farce. His mother had Phillip and Jack to lean on for support. She didn't need him. He would be of no use. The love of her life had been the bane of his existence. He would rather dance on his father's grave than weep.

What on earth was he doing? He wasn't going through with this. "I am not doing this," he said out loud.

Dana looked at him, confused. "But we are almost there. That sign says Three Miles to Knightsbridge Farm."

Chex inhaled. "Boss? Danger slowed down and looked at him curiously.

"We'll drop Dana, then we are going back."

"So, who will I go back to Kingston with?" Dana pouted.

"Phillip and Pearl," Chex said through gritted teeth. He was feeling a little lightheaded as they drove closer to the farm. "Or you can take the bus with the rest of the family."

Dana frowned. "Why do you sound so breathless?"

"Stop the car," Chex said weakly. Danger stopped the car.

Chex closed his eyes. He felt strange like he wasn't getting enough oxygen. Was this a panic attack?

"There is a restaurant up ahead," Danger's voice sounded like it was coming from a distance. It says Silver Spoon Restaurant. Do you want me to leave you there and then come back?"

"Yes," Chex nodded. He kept his eyes closed, willing the feeling to pass.

"It's pretty over here," Dana whistled. "Maybe I should stay with you. Who wants to go to a stuffy old funeral anyway?"

"Go," Chex cracked an eye open. "You came all this way."

"And so did you," Dana said.

"Coming was a mistake," Chex said hoarsely. "I shouldn't have come; this was a bad call by my therapist. It's like returning to the crime scene where you were the victim."

Dana nodded. "So the rumors were true?"

"What rumors?" Chex asked.

"That he tied you up on a cross and whipped you until you couldn't move?" Dana inhaled, "Or that he had a house on the property called Punishment House where he locked you in the dark and starved you until you told him what he wanted to hear?"

"Sounds about right," Chex said, getting out of the car. "That's why I ran away from home at sixteen, and when the police brought me back, I refused to leave the car. They had to take me to the station until Grandpa Eustace came for me."

"Why didn't Laurel do something?" Dana whispered, her eyes bright with unshed tears.

"Whenever she did," Chex said, "he would up my punishment. He didn't want her to love us more than him. He was rabidly jealous of her attention."

"Why didn't she leave?" Dana whispered.

"Because she loved him back," Chex inhaled. "Nothing could shake that love. I have never understood it. Maybe you can ask her when you see her. I don't think I can face her right now or this farce of a funeral."

He slammed the door and headed toward the restaurant. He couldn't recall any of the businesses on the lower part of the hills, except Wimples Bakery, but it made sense that there would be development to cater to the tourists and the locals who lived up in the hills. Maybe when Danger came back, he would take a drive around.

He entered the restaurant, which had a warm and inviting atmosphere and looked like any high-end place in Kingston. As soon as he stepped inside, the smell of fried chicken greeted him. He hadn't tasted good, home-cooked fried chicken in ages. He wasn't even hungry; he had just wanted a break. Now, after smelling the chicken, he definitely would order something. Soft reggae music played in the background, adding to the atmosphere of the place.

As he approached, a hostess greeted him with a warm smile. "Table for one?" she asked politely.

Chex nodded, "Yes, please."

He followed her through the bustling restaurant, the chatter of other patrons providing a temporary reprieve from the heaviness on his mind. He settled into a corner booth; he could see the door from where he was and the gardens where he sat.

His mind kept returning to Dana's question about Laurel. "Why didn't your mother do something?"

He had asked her the same question over the years but never got a satisfactory answer. Why couldn't she have loved them enough to leave Maurice? He had never had a mother's love. Maybe that was why he treated women shabbily.

His therapist, Dr. Henry, would probably tell him he was on the right track, connecting the dots between his tumultuous past and how it shaped his present.

The hostess handed him a menu with a reassuring smile, interrupting the stream of his thoughts for a moment.

"Your server will be right with you. Enjoy your meal."

Chex studied the menu. His mind swirled with childhood memories marked by the absence of a mother's love and his father's cruelty. The question of why Laurel didn't take decisive action to protect her children persisted.

"Neon!" He heard a familiar voice screech at the door. "Halt! Run, don't walk!"

He looked up from the menu, and his heart stopped beating. It felt like it literally stopped pumping blood. Everything was still inside him and around him.

There was Garnet at the restaurant's door —Garnet Silver—the one he had pushed away, the one woman who had made him feel too much and too deeply. He had broken up with her because of that. And she hadn't put up much of a fight, had she?

She had just walked away, and now she was standing at the door of a restaurant that bore her name. Why hadn't it clicked before?

Her hair was longer than he had ever seen it. She was dressed in jeans, shorts, and a tank top and wore large shades—typical Garnet attire. She looked prettier than ever if that was possible.

"Mommy, please, can I have ice cream?" The curly-haired little boy was talking to her. "Mommy, please."

What on earth was going on? Chex straightened up in his seat, shock ricocheting through him. Garnet had a kid?

She must have seen him move, or maybe it was that intense awareness that had always been between them from the moment they met; she looked in his direction and gasped.

He waved to her briefly, affecting a cool he never knew he had within him.

Garnet didn't move. She seemed as if she was contemplating ignoring him. What would she do?

For infinitesimal seconds, he waited to see what she would do, and then she lifted her hand and gave him her middle finger.

He smiled. Nearly six years later, and she was still filled with fire and attitude.

She crouched beside the boy and said something to him, and he followed the cashier around the back.

Then she headed towards his table and sat across from him, perching the sunglasses on her hair.

She was even more beautiful up close, with brown eyes like molten chocolate, lips the shade of a juicy red strawberry, and skin the color of warm caramel; he had always thought she looked like an indulgent treat.

Why had he allowed her to leave him? He had encouraged it even. He had treated her like crap at the end. He had rather done that than face his feelings for her and admit that with her he was in over his head.

"Hey," she said dispassionately, "I didn't expect to see you here."

"Here as in at this particular restaurant or here as in Crimson Hills?" Chex asked, happy that his voice sounded normal.

"Both," Garnet shrugged.

"I came for my father's funeral and had a..." he cleared his throat, "I just couldn't do it."

"Understandable," Garnet nodded. "I am shocked you even made an attempt."

"My therapist thought it would be a splendid idea. I am

going to have to fire him."

"You are in therapy?" Garnet widened her eyes. "Wow."

"It was necessary," Chex leaned back in his seat.

"I know," Garnet chuckled. "If ever there was a candidate for therapy, you were it."

"Are you ready to order?" The waitress came over. Her name tag said, Marie.

"The fried chicken," Chex said, "and whatever sides come with that."

"Do you want anything, Garnet?" Marie asked, looking between the two of them curiously.

"Yes," Garnet nodded, "I want some of Erin's lunch. Tell her to send some out here."

The waitress chuckled.

Chex narrowed his eyes. "Who is Erin?"

"My brother, Garwin's wife. She is also a chef here. I am spending the summer in Crimson Hills; I come here to eat most days. Usually, I have whatever Erin is having; she does the best salads you have ever tasted."

"I didn't remember that your brothers had a restaurant here," Chex said. "It never clicked in my mind when I stopped here that this place was owned by your family. I guess I wasn't thinking, but it's obvious now, the silver in Silver Spoon. "

"Yup," Garnet nodded. "Usually, you are sharper than that."

Chex grimaced. "I am out of sorts today, and to be fair, there are so many changes in this place. I can vaguely recall this spot being a cattle pasture."

"Yes," Garnet said, "things change."

"Like the fact that you have a kid," Chex said, abruptly changing the topic from Crimson Hill and its changes.

"I have a kid," Garnet repeated.

"Why does he look like my brother?" Chex asked, leaning forward.

"Which one of your brothers?" Garnet smirked.

"Phillip," Chex said. "Phillip looks like Dad. Is he Phillip's kid?"

Garnet shook her head. "Guess again."

"He is not Jack's kid," Chex said. "I took Jack to lose his virginity downtown at Dusty's Boudoir nearly two and a half years ago."

"Ew," Garnet chuckled. "I bet Jack found that horrifying."

"He found his wife there," Chex said.

"Are you serious?" Garnet laughed.

"It's a long story," Chex said, "it turns out she had links in Crimson Hills, too, and she wasn't really a prostitute at all. It's been two years, and I still have to apologize to her occasionally for misjudging her."

"Serves you right," Garnet laughed.

"I tried to keep them apart," Chex said, "I guess I deserve it."

The waitress brought the food. It smelled and looked good. She also brought a plate of salad for Garnet, which looked like a colorful work of art.

"It tastes as good as it looks, trust me," Garnet murmured. "Be still, my heart; it's a steak cobb salad with blue cheese and broccoli."

"So whose kid is he?" Chex asked before she could dig in.

"He is mine," Garnet said.

"Which one of my cousins did you sleep with?" Chex asked. "It's really puzzling; he has a Knight face with Hastings eyes. It would have to be someone who is related to both my dad and my mom."

"Mmm," Garnet said, "I wonder who that could be. I can't think of anyone who I had sex with who is related to both of 'your' parents, who could possibly be a candidate?"

"You got birth control injections, and I wore a condom every time," Chex said.

"He was conceived that weekend, a couple of months after we broke up. We both missed each other, but you were adamant that we had to make a clean break after the weekend because you would eventually hurt me," Garnet drizzled dressing over her salad. "Nothing could convince you otherwise. And I was done begging you to give us a chance."

"I remember you accepted my speech and left," Chex nodded. He didn't want to remember. She had been calm and matter-of-fact and handled the breakup like a pro. He, on the other hand, had been so emotional that he had even scared himself.

"So he is mine?" He managed to ask out loud.

"No, he is not," Garnet said patiently. "He is mine. You can forget you ever saw him and move on with your life. I know your thoughts on children; I do not want him to find out that his sperm donor would not want him. I weighed the pros and cons of telling you about Neon in the past, and the cons outweighed the pros."

"You named him Neon," Chex murmured. He didn't bother to deny her conclusion about wanting children. He had always made that abundantly clear.

"I always liked that name," Garnet said.

"Yes, I remember," Chex looked across the parking lot. His appetite had fled, and he felt vestiges of that breathlessness he had felt earlier.

Thankfully, Danger drove in before the feeling could spread and overwhelm him like before. This day sucked on so many levels; he wasn't happy that he was seeing Garnet in this state, and he was slightly shocked that he was a father.

He needed a breather. He needed time to process all of this.

Chapter Two

"I'll take this to go," Chex said. He raised his hand, and the waitress came over. "This has been a bit too much," he said when the waitress left with his plate.

Garnet swallowed. Why had she expected a different reaction? This was Chex, damaged, and maybe beyond repair.

He had never made any excuses about what kind of person he was. She had known and gotten involved with him anyway. She had his child, knowing that she would be parenting alone.

"I get it," she said hoarsely. "This is like emotional overload, today of all the days."

Was it pathetic to want to ask him when she would see him again? But she knew that look in Chex's eyes he was shutting down. And when Chex shut down, he needed his space. He was like a turtle completely withdrawing into his shell, only pushing his head out again when he felt emotionally strong.

She had learned that about him while they were together. Chex didn't process emotional matters quickly or easily. She studied him furtively. He looked the same, maybe a little more muscular, but it was the same Chex, light caramel complexion, light brown eyes that held a quiet intensity, and a smile that could disarm even the most guarded heart. He had cut his hair, he used to wear it in long plaits, and he had a circular beard mustache that was neatly trimmed, giving him a more mature look.

There was an unspoken tension between them, a residue of unresolved emotions that lingered from their encounter five years ago.

As she observed him, memories flooded back, both sweet and bitter. Their shared laughter, the inside jokes only they understood, and the warmth of his presence were juxtaposed against the pain of their parting.

The atmosphere crackled with the unsaid, hanging heavy like a storm about to break. She debated whether to confront the past or let the silence persist.

The decision weighed on her, a delicate balance between risking vulnerability and maintaining the carefully constructed walls around her heart.

Marie returned with his food in a takeout box while Garnet still worried about what to say that would sound wise and nonchalant.

Nothing was forthcoming.

Chex stood up. "I'll see you around, Garnet."

He left a wad of cash on the table.

Garnet nodded. She wouldn't be seeing him. Chex didn't like Crimson Hills, and he was not readily accessible in Kingston—not that she would ever approach him for anything.

She watched him as he sauntered to the door, looking for

all the world like a man living through a nightmare.

She inhaled once and then twice. She had gotten over Chex and her inexplicable reactions to him long ago.

She continued eating her salad. She would not waste a brain cell mulling over the walking complexity that was Chex.

"This is a wad of cash from your gentleman friend. Is this a tip?" Marie asked, breaking her out of her contemplations.

"We have never been friends," Garnet muttered. "Of course, it's a tip! Has Garwin left with Neon yet?"

"Yes, they're gone," Marie nodded.

"I'm going to head out," Garnet said, looking down at what was left of her salad. Could you pack this to go for me, please?"

"Sure," Marie nodded. "You okay?"

"I am fine,"

 Garnet smiled at Marie, "Thanks for asking."

Marie nodded, but obviously, she didn't believe her. It was no surprise that Gersham texted her when she was leaving.

"Who is the man that made you sad?"

Garnet smiled. Marie probably went to the kitchen and announced that a heavy tipper made Garnet sad.

Gersham and Erin were probably preparing the food for Maurice Knight's repast, yet he was concerned about her.

"Neon's father." She texted back.

He sent her back a shocked face emoji and then said, "Come around the back, let's chat.

I thought you were busy. Garnet texted, you have several events today.

True, Gersham said. Tell me all about it at our family meeting tomorrow at the house at four."

"Which house?" Garnet texted back. Since they had gotten back Silver Manor, they had two places to call 'the' house.

Leonard Crooks had completely transformed their father's childhood home into four three-bedroom luxury townhouses and had rented them out as high-end accommodations. It had an Olympic-sized pool, a cabana, and all the luxurious details for which clients pay top dollar.

After seeing what Silver Manor was like, she had opted to spend the summer in Crimson Hills. It was like living at a hotel—they even had staff!

It hadn't quite sunken in how drastically their fortunes had changed. The Silvers had moved up from the poorest family in Crimson Hills to owning the most luxurious abode in the small town. Leonard Crooks had spared no expense in renovating the place.

After killing her grandmother and fraudulently adjusting her will to leave everything for himself, Leonard made everything better in the end. The house and property were vastly improved, and the business had grown a hundredfold since the Silvers had it.

It was poetic justice at its finest. Her father and aunt were rightfully reinstated as the true owners of everything they had lost, but now things were far better than they were before.

The one house now had four villas, and each had a name: gold, silver, platinum, and palladium; Leonard Crooks had quite unironically made a play with their metallic surname and named the villas.

In the brochure that she had seen in her villa, the promotional pamphlet had said: these metals are highly resistant to corrosion, paragons of endurance, standing as unwavering guardians against the elements of time and uncertainty. Each villa is a sanctuary where luxury meets durability. We will always be here as a luxurious retreat to satisfy your every need.

When they first read it, Garnet, Patti, and Erin giggled over the description. Her brothers had been too in awe of the place to find the humor in the description.

With their father's blessing, they decided to move to the villas instead of continuing to use them for income.

Gersham had put the villa names in a hat, and the siblings and Joy, acting on Sterling's behalf, had chosen which villa each would claim.

Garnet had chosen Villa Platinum, and she was quite pleased with it. She liked the greyish-white platinum accents in the villa's decor.

For now, she and Neon were the only ones fully moved in. That would soon change, though. Garwin and Erin were almost fully moved into the Villa Palladium. Gersham and Patti had just returned from their world tour and would be moving soon. Her father was due out of rehab next week, and his former home was the first place he would see. It would be good for him to be in a new environment away from the old memories of their former home.

She had quite forgotten that she had asked Gersham a question. She slid into her car and started it for the AC. This summer was going to be hot if mid-May was any indication.

"Silver Manor," Gersham texted her back. "Aunt Joy is on her way to Crimson Hills for a two-week vacation, so it's a good time for a family meeting."

True. Garnet thought. Aunt Joy was only coming for a supposed vacation to check up on Neon. She didn't completely trust Garnet with his care.

Somewhere along the way, she had given up parental control of Neon to her aunt without batting an eyelid. Now that she was back, her aunt found it hard to let go.

"Can you plan a party for Dad's return?" Gersham texted. "And tell us what you have in mind at the meeting."

Garnet frowned and texted back. "I have no time to plan a party. We'll just have food and non-alcoholic drinks and sit poolside and chat; Dad is not the sociable type. He'll be fine. I must come up with a topic and an outline for a documentary for my final project."

"Are you still on that?" Gersham asked.

"Yes," Garnet texted. "I am torn between featuring the history of Crimson Hill Great House or the time travel myth of the Great House."

"Time travel," Gersham texted back.

Of course, he'd say that. Garnet smiled. Every great house had its particular mythology. The well-known Rose Hall Great House had the White Witch, Annie Palmer. To this day, people are still fascinated by the stories they made up to make the place interesting.

Surely, she could feature Crimson Hill Great House and their made-up time travel stories; it would be interesting and probably captivate various age groups. She could also sample some classical music and put a modern spin on it to satisfy all the project requirements.

Whatever she decided to do, she had to do it soon. She had a deadline to submit her project outline by the beginning of June.

She started the car. That's what she was going to focus on. She was finally getting her degree because she hated not finishing something she started. The timing was right.

This was the summer when she would get to know her son properly, and he could get to know her. It was just the two of them, no Aunt Joy to pick up the slack. They were getting used to each other.

Neon had an excellent summer school program at Crimson Hill Prep, which included swimming, football practice, and horseback riding. He was busy and happy, adjusting to living with her without a glitch. She was grateful for that. Neon had been so attached to her aunt she had thought the transition of her being around him full-time would have been harder. But her boy was a trooper. They had just about settled on a workable routine, and it had no space for Chex Hastings.

How could she not think about Chex for the rest of the week?

After seeing Chex, it was as if her world had lit up. She had felt something, a spark of excitement that only Chex had invoked in her. It would be hell in the coming days when she ran the meeting repeatedly in her mind. Eventually, she would run herself ragged.

She backed out of the parking lot and started up the hill, driving slowly as she digested that she had seen Chex again today. For all intents and purposes, their meeting today would be a one-off, a blip on her radar, a story she would tell Neon when he was older.

"Yes, I actually saw your biological father when you were little, and he knows about you, but he didn't show any interest in either of us. Things are what they are and can't be helped." She exhaled tremulously when she thought of that.

She didn't grow up with a father and turned out quite fine. After Sterling returned from jail, she was a teenager living with her aunt in Kingston. Their first meeting after coming to Crismon Hills for the summer had been a dud. It was apparent that they would not have a good relationship. Sterling had sat and stared at her, not answering one question she asked or participating in the conversation. He had looked through her like all the lights were on and nobody was home.

She had never had an adult conversation with her father through the years. They exchanged pleasantries, no heart-to-heart talks, no deep conversations. They were basically strangers who shared DNA.

Sterling was like a placeholder in her life, whom she called dad, not because of any fondness on her part, but because Gersham and Garwin called him that.

She didn't miss him growing up; she had her big brothers, Gersham and Garwin, who had fulfilled a fatherly role in her life at various times.

They were excellent big brothers and even better uncles. Neon would not be bereft of male guidance.

One day, she would find someone she could love as deeply as she had loved Chex. And maybe then Neon would have a father figure living with them. Garnet sighed; that was a hard possibility.

She had sailed the globe in the past two years as a cruise ship singer, and she hadn't met anyone who had even remotely piqued her interest. She was a case of arrested emotional development. What was it about Chex Hastings that had been so magnetic?

She drove to the house, waited for the automatic gate to open, and seriously pondered the question. And then she got her answer.

Underneath Chex Hastings's cool-as-cucumber attitude and laid-back exterior existed a genuine, nonjudgmental, friendly person who didn't play games and was brutally honest. He somehow effortlessly made her feel valued; he was genuinely interested in her as a person, not just for her looks.

And he got her. He really did.

She headed for the pool area. She would indulge herself in thinking about the past, just this once, and then she would bottle back the memories and squeeze them into the far recesses of her brain.

Chapter Three

Sometime in the Past

"This is nice," Garnet whispered to Arlene after they settled at the back of the 150-seat concert hall at Right Vibes Studio. They were there to audition for DJ Duke's first studio album as backup singers. They had both signed up for the audition when it was advertised at their respective schools and were chosen to audition before the producers live.

It was a happy coincidence for her, Garnet thought. At least she had someone to hang with while she waited to audition. Arlene lived a few houses from her aunt's place. They had gone to the same high school and had even carpooled together. They had both sung in the school choir.

Arlene had chosen to attend college in Kingston after high school. Garnet had chosen college in Montego Bay so that she could spend more time with her brothers in Crimson Hill and work as a singer on the hotel circuit in Jamaica. She had three hotels, which she rotated through every summer.

This was the first summer since she had hit sixteen that she was not working. Usually, as soon as school went on summer break, she worked full-time as a singer. When school was in session, she only worked three nights per week and all weekend. She was constantly on call because they loved her voice, and the pay was good. She had made enough money to buy her own car, pay for her college expenses, and build an additional wing on their childhood house with Gersham.

This audition to be a background vocalist for the hottest singer around wasn't about money; it would be a considerable career boost. She wouldn't have to audition for any singing gigs again. People would call her. She would be booked and busy and rolling in dough.

And if she was chosen to tour with DJ Duke, that would be a huge boon. She would quit or delay her final year in college for that; it would be a once-in-a-lifetime experience.

She was doing her degree in Music and Film Studies; this would be a practical experience that could not be replicated in the classroom.

Garnet rubbed her fingers along the ticket and looked around the concert hall. So many people were auditioning, and this was day three. She had seen the flyer on the music department noticeboard and sent a video of her singing, as requested. She was given a date, and here she was, her first time in an actual production house.

Right Vibes did not only do music production; they also did film production. This would be the perfect place to work after school; they did exactly what she liked.

She spotted a brochure on a seat to her left, and she picked it up. They needed to restock the lobby with the brochures, since many persons had passed through in the last couple of days. Maybe they hadn't gotten around to it yet.

"Read that out loud," Arlene said. "I was wondering where

those went."

"Ehem," Garnet cleared her throat. "Right Vibes Productions was founded by the visionary Chex Hastings and is a force to be reckoned with in the realms of music, documentaries, music videos, and short films. At the tender age of eighteen, Chex Hastings embarked on a journey fueled by passion, creativity, and an unyielding belief in the transformative power of storytelling.

"Right Vibes Productions prides itself on its diverse portfolio, seamlessly transitioning between the auditory and visual realms. From soul-stirring musical compositions that transcend genres to thought-provoking documentaries that challenge perspectives, Right Vibes Productions is a testament to the limitless boundaries of creativity.

"The music division at Right Vibes Productions boasts some top international artists in its stable. From chart-topping hits to experimental soundscapes, the company's commitment to pushing musical boundaries has garnered a dedicated fan base. Renowned for discovering and nurturing emerging talents, Right Vibes Productions is not just a production company but a launchpad for the stars of tomorrow."

"Oh wow," Arlene said.

"Yup, I am impressed," Garnet nodded. "Chex started all of this at eighteen. That's remarkable."

There was a picture of him in the brochure. She studied it intently.

"He's cute. No, scrap that. He is handsome. Look at his eyes—they are an unusual color and kind of dreamy, and his lips are dark pink and juicy-looking. He looks like he just needs to raise an eyebrow, and the women come running."

Arlene snorted with laughter. "You are not wrong."

"I love a man who wears his hair in cornrows."

"Yep, me too," Arlene said.

"And he is so muscular," Garnet continued her thirsty assessment of the producer. "He should have taken off his shirt for the picture."

"Girl, you need to stop," Arlene chuckled, "Chex Hastings is an untamable bad boy. He only sleeps with prostitutes, call girls, and go-go dancers. He doesn't do relationships. You are not his type."

"You don't know that," Garnet said.

"Your body count is probably under five," Arlene snickered. He likes his bed partners to be very experienced."

"My body count is zero, actually," Garnet said. "I have never kissed anyone."

"Never?" Arlene widened her eyes.

"Never," Garnet nodded.

"Well, you are as good as invisible to Chex, then," Arlene chuckled.

"How do you know this?" Garnet asked.

"My cousin Danger works for him as his security guard and driver," Arlene said. "The first time I saw Chex was at Danger's birthday bash. I was awestruck and crushing on him so hard."

Arlene leaned back in her chair with a sigh.

"And?" Garnet asked.

"And Danger laughed at me, told me the same thing I just told you."

"Is your cousin's name really Danger?" Garnet asked.

"Yes," Arlene nodded.

"And you all call him Danger, not Dane or Dan?"

Arlene chuckled, "Yes. He doesn't like his name shortened."

"What's his middle name?"

"Conrad," Arlene said.

"Your aunt and uncle must be fascinating people," Garnet murmured. "Do they have other children?"

"Yes, but their names are not as remarkable. Danger's brothers are Able and Noble, and his sister's name is Blithe," Arlene smiled. "They were really going in with the adjective names. I quite like Danger, though."

"I wonder what Chex means," Garnet mused.

"It's cereal, duh," Arlene chuckled.

"When I get the gig, I will ask him," Garnet said.

"I like the confidence," Arlene nodded. "But I can't help but think we are wasting our time. They must have chosen their backup singers a long time ago. This is the last day; they only have us here because they feel obligated to go through the list."

"You have to change that attitude," Garnet said, "or you'll sabotage yourself before entering the sound room. I wonder if Chex will be in there."

"More than likely," Arlene said. "DJ Duke is his artiste. Chex discovered him and is grooming him to be an international sensation, and this project is personal. I heard he wrote all the songs on the new album."

"All the songs?" Garnet widened her eyes.

"Yep," Arlene nodded.

"He is handsome and creative," Garnet whispered.

"And troubled, and only sleeps with women he pays, he parties hard, drinks like a fish, smokes like a chimney, and he thinks women are to be seen, not heard," Arlene added. "Get your feet back on the ground, Garnet. Do not develop a crush on Chex Hastings; he is bad news."

"Whoa," Garnet looked at her. "That was rather harsh, but I hear you."

****

Garnet was in the last batch of singers to audition, and it was nearly six o'clock before she went into the inner studio. It had been a long day's wait, and she had almost given up. But this was a world-renowned studio; they put artists on the map. She would have been foolish to leave just because she had to wait a little.

Arlene had gotten through hours before and had called to tell her that it was a simple process. "You sing, they listen, everybody is pleasant. They'll let everyone know who is in or out by tomorrow."

"Who is 'they'?" Garnet had asked.

"Chex, the producer, DJ Duke, the artist, and Croy, the engineer, and the A&R rep for Right Vibes. Her name is Lexi; she's mean and has a phony American accent. Watch out for her."

Lexi greeted Garnet at the door. "So sorry to have you waiting. Are you familiar with a sound booth?"

Garnet nodded. "I am."

"Great," Lexi smiled. Her smile was mostly gums; she had itty-bitty teeth. "We want to hear your take on DJ Duke's song, 'No Promises.'"

Lexi didn't sound or come off mean, Garnet thought. And her accent was not phony. She must have done something to rub Arlene the wrong way.

Garnet stepped into the sound booth. It was well-lit inside. The equipment and controls were neatly arranged, and the acoustics seemed top-notch. She took a deep breath, feeling a mix of excitement and nerves. This was her chance to showcase her talent in a world-class studio.

She put on the headphones and adjusted the microphone. She saw the four individuals on the other side of the glass window. Her eyes connected with Chex's, and she suddenly felt nervous. They were all observing her, waiting for her to start. She dragged her eyes away from Chex's; the stare between them had been so intense. How many girls had thought that today, though?

Before she could lose focus, the instrumental track of "No Promises" began playing in her ears. Garnet closed her eyes to immerse herself in the music. Music was the ultimate de-stressor for her, her comfort, her friend. She was going to nail this.

Her voice resonated through the sound booth as she poured emotion into every lyric. The melody filled the studio, and Garnet lost herself in the moment, forgetting the long wait and the anxiety that had accompanied it.

"In the city lights where shadows dance, whispers in the wind taking a chance. Walking down the street, lost in reverie. No promises tonight, just you and me."

After the last note faded, Garnet opened her eyes to see the panel nodding in approval. Lexi was smiling wide, revealing those tiny teeth once more.

"That was impressive, Garnet," Chex remarked, his voice raspy and deep. It actually sent shivers down her spine. She knew she was looking at him with a helplessness in her expression; she had to force herself to look away.

"DJ Duke, what do you think?" Chex asked. He was still looking at her; she could feel his eyes on her, even while talking to the people around him.

DJ Duke nodded in approval, "I like her vibe. She adds something special to the song."

Croy, the engineer, chimed in, "Clean vocals, great control. This could work well in the mix."

Lexi, still smiling, though slightly less gummy, spoke up, "We'll be in touch by tomorrow to let you know the final decision. Thank you for coming in."

Garnet inhaled deeply. They liked her, right? Or did

everybody get this pleasant review after every audition?

She left the studio on cloud nine and went to her car; the key would not turn over in the ignition. She sat there for nearly half an hour fussing with the thing. One of the security guards came over to inquire about it and she ended up calling her aunt, who called her mechanic friend, who told her to sit tight; he was on his way.

Her belly grumbled, and she felt slightly headachy; she hadn't eaten all day. She put her head on the steering wheel and took deep breaths; these things happened, cars had issues, and people were inconvenienced all the time.

"What's wrong?" She knew it was Chex who asked; his voice was so sexy he could read a directory and make your toes curl.

She looked up to see him standing by her car, his light eyes glowing like honey gold in the late evening sun. He was studying her with a mix of concern and curiosity.

"The car won't start. My key won't turn in the ignition," Garnet explained, feeling a bit embarrassed about the situation.

"Let me give it a try," Chex said. He leaned down and shifted the steering wheel left and right.

To Garnet's surprise, the engine roared to life with a simple turn of the key when Chex attempted to start it. She stared at him in disbelief. "But…it didn't start when I tried it!"

"Sometimes, it just needs a gentle touch," he said, offering a reassuring smile. There was no sexual innuendo in his voice at all, and yet she felt a tingle down her spine.

"Thank you so much," Garnet tried to keep the tremor out of her voice. With him so near, she could smell his perfume and almost feel the warmth of his skin. It was doing crazy things to her insides.

"Garnet Silver," Chex smiled, "you have an artist name,

you know that?"

"It's the Silver. It works with most things," Garnet said inanely.

He gestured toward the studio. "We were all impressed in there. Your audition was something special.

"We'll be in touch tomorrow, but I have a feeling you'll be hearing good news," Chex said. He was straightening up to leave when her belly made the loudest, most embarrassing rumble.

He looked at her and chuckled, "You are cordially invited to share dinner with me if you want."

Garnet closed her eyes. "I am so embarrassed. I should go."

"It's a lot of food, and today's menu sounded really good," Chex said. "We at Right Vibes are always willing to share."

"Okay," Garnet nodded, "I'll have to call the mechanic and tell him not to bother."

****

She ended up in the staff dining room, which was quite big and had more people than she had expected. The food was laid out buffet-style. Chex was right; it was a lot of food.

Lexi, DJ Duke, and Croy were sitting at a table eating and huddled together, Garnet observed. No doubt they were discussing the day's events. They didn't look surprised to see her with Chex.

Lexi waved to her and then went back to talking with her group. She was definitely not mean; Arlene had got that wrong.

There were several other people at their tables, eating and chatting.

"Who are they?" Garnet whispered.

"The staff," Chex said. "We have several projects running concurrently at the moment. We usually work late into the evening here. This is not a traditional nine-to-five company."

Garnet nodded. "I expected that."

"Come and join me over there when you get your food," Chex said, pointing to a table where a man sat. That's Sam, the studio manager. He oversees the day-to-day operations of this place. He frees me up so I can focus on any creative project I find interesting."

Garnet nodded. Sam was seriously handsome; he looked like he could be a model of some sort—narrow features, dark skin, shaven head. She couldn't guess his age. He also looked serious, as if he didn't smile much. He appeared a little intimidating from where she was standing.

Garnet took a deep breath. This was amazing; she would have dinner with the owner and manager of Right Vibes studio. Would she even manage to eat?

Her belly rumbled a resounding yes. She chose a little of everything and went over to the table.

Chex looked into her plate and nodded approvingly. She had piled it high.

"Samuel Lewis, this is Garnet Silver. She auditioned today for a spot on DJ Duke's album."

"Ah," Sam smiled. "Nice to meet you, Garnet. You are quite pretty."

"Thank you," Garnet lifted her fork.

"Tell me about yourself," Sam said.

"Let her eat," Chex said lazily. "She was waiting here all day, and then her car wouldn't start when she was supposed to leave."

"Oh," Sam smiled. "And Chex rescued you."

"He did," Garnet said. "Not a minute too soon; I was

perishing of hunger."

"How old are you?" Sam asked.

"Twenty on the twenty-ninth of February." Garnet took her first bite of food and closed her eyes. It was good. She forced herself to eat at a reasonable pace.

"You are a leaper?" Sam asked.

"I am," Garnet nodded.

"So, which day do you celebrate when there isn't a leap year?"

"I celebrate for the whole month," Garnet said. "I actually have a birth month celebration."

"I like that," Sam chuckled.

Garnet's eyes collided with Chex's. He hadn't said a word; he was observing her interaction with Sam.

"And where do you work?" Sam asked.

"I sing at various hotels," Garnet answered between bites, "but I also attend school full time. I am doing my degree in Music and Film Studies. I am interested in the production side of things."

"Oh really," Chex finally spoke.

"Yes," Garnet nodded. "I love everything about the production process. I sing because I can, and people seem to like my voice, but my passion lies in production: putting the raw material together, adding the appropriate music, making a documentary, movie, or even an ad, knowing that I can put it in a format for people to enjoy. That's what I really want to do."

"That's interesting; when did this passion begin?" Sam leaned forward,

"From a young age, I have always been fascinated with behind-the-scenes footage. There was this program called Behind The Scenes that used to come on in the evenings. They had interviews with the guys in the background, the movie makers you do not see. They'd show you a little bit of what goes into making a show. I was awed by how many people it took to make it happen. I wanted to be one of those people. I wasn't quite sure what area to go in." Garnet continued, "And then one evening they interviewed a music supervisor, a freelancer who had worked on so many television shows they only listed the major ones, and she was explaining the process, and I said, that's what I want to do. That's it, that's exactly it!"

"Sounds like you have a lot in common with Chex," Sam chuckled.

"We do?" She looked at Chex, who just smiled wryly.

"Yes, he can sing too, quite well," Sam said, "but he prefers production. You two should explore this some more. Is this your first time at a production house?"

"Yes," Garnet tried to avoid looking directly at Chex again. Was she the only one feeling this pull between them?

Chex didn't seem bothered by any attraction between them whatsoever.

"I'll give you a tour of the facilities when you are done eating," Chex offered casually. "Excuse me a moment; I have a call to make."

He left her with Sam, and she felt bereft when he left the table. Sam peppered her with questions about school, life, and family, which she answered politely, only perking up again when Chex returned to the table with his food.

He ended up giving her a tour, which was cut short when one of his staff asked for an opinion. Garnet stood by while they chatted. And then Chex looked up, "It's getting late. I should walk you to your car. This is going to take a while. We'll take a rain check on the tour."

So she would be back, she smiled.

"What does your name mean?" She had mustered up the

courage to ask.

"As far as I know, it doesn't have a meaning. It's a compilation of my mother's grandparents' names, Cheryl and Alex Hastings."

"Oh," Garnet nodded, "that's cute."

They stared at each other for an interminable amount of time before he said, "Goodnight, Garnet."

"Goodnight, Chex."

****

Garnet snapped out of her trip down memory lane when her phone rang. It was Garwin.

"Say, Garnet, can you come for Neon? He is injured."

"What?" Garnet gasped. "You just took him to practice! What's wrong with my baby? I knew football was too rough for him."

Garwin chuckled. "Your baby didn't even start playing; he stubbed his toe on a stone before he could get a kick in. I can't leave the other boys, or I would take him home."

"Is he crying?" Garnet asked.

"He was," Garwin said, "but now he is calmer and wants to play. But I wouldn't want him to agitate the toe."

"Okay, I am coming," Garnet got up.

It was back to reality for her and back to her everyday life. Her memories of her and Chex would have to wait for another time.

Chapter Four

"**F**ollow her car," Chex said to Danger when they saw Garnet driving from the restaurant parking lot. "Don't let her see you."

Chex had dithered in the parking lot, torn between leaving and staying to hear more about Garnet and his son. He had a son. Just the very statement was unreal to him. Two years ago, he had a vasectomy to avoid having a child. When he had one all along, he didn't know how to feel about it.

"I didn't know the lovely Garnet was back in the picture," Danger murmured. "You once said she unleashed your madness."

"I saw her quite by accident today. She had a kid; it's mine," Chex said out loud.

Danger looked around at him. "My condolences."

Chex chuckled. "The kid looks like my dad, a miniature version of him. This kind of thing makes me believe that God has a sense of humor."

"Well, if you were made in God's image, it stands to reason that he does have some humor since you have one," Danger said philosophically.

"I couldn't go to the man's funeral, and now I have a kid that looks like him," Chex sighed. "How was the funeral going anyway when you dropped Dana off?"

"Knightsbridge is the prettiest farm I have ever been to," Danger said. "I like it. The church is in a nice spot."

"I know where it is," Chex snorted. "I had to attend every day when my abuser was alive."

Danger cleared his throat. "The funeral was well attended even though it's a weekday. It's shocking how many people were there."

"Knightsbridge is a large farm with nearly fifty full-time staff and seasonal workers." Chex said, "They would attend, and there are so many more who left or are retired. My father was responsible for all of their livelihood. Knightsbridge is a community within a community. It was designed so you didn't have to leave, except for a serious health condition."

"I would live there," Danger murmured. "I wonder if I could get a job? They have tight security; I had to declare my weapon and show them my permit to carry before they let me through. I wonder if Jack wants one more security personnel. I would work security, settle down with one of the robust-looking country ladies I saw at the church, and have a couple of children roaming the countryside."

Chex chuckled. "I could imagine you and a robust country lady."

"What's the housing like?" Danger asked.

"Free," Chex said.

"And the benefits?"

"Standard," Chex sighed. "Are you going to tell me more about the funeral, or are you going to blatantly search for another job when you are in my employ?"

Danger laughed. "When I got there, it seemed to be winding down. Dana immediately went over to a group of people. They were chatting and laughing it up outside under a tent that was erected to handle the overflow from the church."

"Did you see my brothers?" Chex asked.

"Yep, I saw Jack; he was outside," Danger said. "He was shocked to see me. I told him you tried to make it; he said to tell you you're not missing anything. It's all a bunch of hypocritical nonsense, anyway. He said he had to take a step outside before he snapped."

Chex smiled. "That's my boy. Well, that makes me feel loads better. I can't imagine what nice things anyone would say about my father. I'd probably hear the lies and leave."

"People can be both nice and evil," Danger said. "One of your father's workers' sons was speaking when I got there. He was describing how generous and kind your father was. He said your father sent him and all his siblings to school, up to college. One was a doctor, one a lawyer, one an engineer, and one owned a business. They were all doing well, thanks to Maurice Knight."

"Ironic, isn't it?" Chex huffed. "My father tried to keep us out of school when I was younger."

Danger stopped because Garnet slowed down and drove into a place that looked like a resort. It had 'Silver Manor' on the gate.

"So they had gotten back their family property," Chex remembered when she told him about her father losing the place to Leonard Crooks after Leonard had married their grandmother, who mysteriously died and left everything to him.

"What should I do?" Danger turned around and looked at

him.

"We go back home," Chex murmured. "But first, we check out the area. So much has changed in twenty years. Drive up to the great house; I want to say hello to Maud. Who knows when I'll come this way again."

Danger started the car, and Chex took in his surroundings. There were so many new houses; the place seemed more refined. He had not left the farm much when he lived in Crimson Hills. He had three years of high school, and then his father had yanked him out to be schooled along with the other children in the cult because he believed the end was nigh. The end was always nigh.

Before high school, he had not been allowed to leave the farm. He remembered vividly his first time leaving Knightsbridge. His grandfather Eustace had come to visit. It was the first time Chex had seen him. He was a tall, light-skinned man with light brown eyes, the same shade as his own. Grandpa Eustace had tears in his eyes after hugging him.

Chex still remembered that bear hug; all the love transferred to his scrawny frame. He was nine years old at the time; Phillip was fourteen, and Jack was just a baby. His grandfather had come to see the new baby.

His mother had proudly said he came after each of them was born. Maurice didn't like outsiders on his farm, but he made an exception for his father-in-law. Eustace had insisted on taking Chex and Phillip out for a drive. Maurice had not put up much of a fight, nor had he sent one of his men with them to ensure they came back.

His grandfather had driven through the gates of Knightsbridge, and Chex had sat in the back seat, looking from side to side, taking it all in. Phillip and his grandfather had carried on a long, tense conversation, with his grandfather muttering at intervals.

"I should just take you two to Kingston now. I can't believe Laurel is allowing that man to actually imprison her and you boys in the bushes. I can't believe you are not attending a high school with children your age, Phillip. This boggles the mind. Laurel is college-educated; she is my only child. Your father has turned her into a simpleton."

"Would you like a soda, Chex?" his grandfather had asked, slowing down at a sign that said Wimples Bakery. "And maybe some other treat."

"What's a soda?" Chex had asked innocently.

Eustace struggled to explain. Chex discovered, though, that it was a fizzy drink that tickled his nose when he drank it. That day, his grandfather had driven slowly up the neighborhood's hills and stopped at Crimson Hill Great House. It had not been a tour day.

They were greeted by a woman who introduced herself as Maud Beecher. She had greeted their grandfather warmly; they had met sometime before. She walked with them to a gazebo that looked out at the sea below. He didn't think he closed his mouth during the entire walk.

"It's his first time coming out of those hills," Maud had murmured behind him. "I think Maurice has several screws loose with his little doomsday cult, and I think the people that follow him are equally crazy."

Phillip and his grandfather chuckled.

"I was thinking of taking Phillip and Chex to Kingston," Eustace sighed heavily. "I am torn. I don't want to kidnap my own grandchildren, but I am seriously considering it. What do you think, Maud? I heard you know the future."

"Maurice's little cult will soon disband," Maud said. "He'll make a business out of the farm eventually and will do well. One day, Jack will run that business."

"What about me?" Phillip had asked eagerly.

"You will escape in a few years," Maud replied. "Your grandfather here will force them to send all of you to school. You will have some years of regular high school; you'll do well, and you'll leave after that."

"How will I force Maurice to send them to school?" Eustace asked tiredly. "Have you ever tried talking to the man? He talks in Bible verses; his whole outlook is doom and gloom."

"Yes," Maud nodded. "But he is not a law unto himself. He still lives in Jamaica, and every child in this country is entitled to an education, and I don't mean the nonsense he and Laurel are teaching them up in the hills. You are a big, rich man, Eustace. Do something for your grandchildren. Threaten him, send the police up there to go poking around in their little cult. Do something that will make him uncomfortable enough to send them to regular school."

Eustace inhaled sharply. "Maybe what I should do is take them with me. I am not leaving these children with Maurice. That man is abusive, locking a child up in the dark, feeding him fruit and water, forcing a growing boy to fast and repent of his sins. What sins? What Maurice is doing is child abuse."

"Whatever you are doing, make sure it is legal," Maud sighed. "Maurice will send his little band of foot soldiers after you. They are armed and radicalized to follow him and only him; he is their messiah. You need to be alive to rescue the children when it's time. All three of them will eventually leave."

"Are you sure about this, Maud?" Eustace asked.

"Yes," Maud nodded. "They will all end up okay, even Chex, though he will suffer the most."

"I don't want Chex to suffer; I'll take him now," Eustace

said. "I can't, with all conscience, leave him in that situation."

"If you take Chex now, it won't go well for the other two," Maud said. "All three of them will eventually get out. Just give it time. Chex will manage; he'll thrive. Chex is a fighter."

****

The great house gates were opened.

"Should I drive in?" Danger looked at him in the rearview mirror.

"Yes," Chex sighed. "I am just going to say a quick hello to Maud."

Through the years before he had the guts to run away for good, he used to visit Maud at Crimson Hill Great House after school before returning to the farm. He couldn't stay too long or visit too often because he didn't want to make his father suspicious.

Maud used to feed him and allow him to experience a bit of normalcy when he visited; they had a little reading club thing going on, just the two of them. She had found some diaries belonging to Winter Wesson, the man who had built Crimson Hill Great House, and she used to read them with eager fascination. She had him reading the stories to her for their entertainment.

The diaries were unexpectedly exciting; he had found Winter's adventures fascinating. He had sailed worldwide, hunting artifacts and indulging in hair-raising adventures. It was more intriguing than anything he had read at school. He had been especially fascinated with Winter's poetry, which he had littered throughout his stories. He especially liked the poem "Not Afraid of The Dark," which he had coined when his ship was wrecked on an island in the Pacific with a tribe of cannibals.

He and his crew had only managed to ward them off with their technology of the day. The savages, as Winter called them, were wary of eating them because they had developed a peculiar device that emitted bright light, which they used to scare off the cannibals. It was a makeshift torch crafted from salvaged ship parts and a concoction of chemicals that produced a brilliant flame.

One night, it rained heavily, and there was no bright light. Winter and his men huddled in the lower cabin of their ship; it was pitch black, the storm was howling around them, and the cannibals could strike at any moment without the light. And Winter had written a poem that had transcended time and space.

"In the dark, I found my light, A glow that banished deepest night."

He had Maud to thank for introducing him to Winter Wesson's works. He owed his resilience to that particular poem, his stories, and maybe even his current career as a producer. He had put music to the poem on the old piano his father had discarded in punishment house. It had been his only company in the dark. He had taught himself to use it; his first produced piece had been Winter Wesson's poem.

Then, he created his own poems, visualizing the notes, the harmony, and the chords in the dark. The last piece he composed before he escaped Knightsbridge was a Winter Wesson poem called "Escape."

"I have to flee to live, I have so much to this world to give…"

It had lit a fire deep inside him. Who knew that an 18th-century historian and poet would have been instrumental in making him leave his home at any cost.

His escape had been funny, too. His father's sister, Reba,

had moved to Knightsbridge to run the farm shop that was turning out to be quite popular among the locals and the hotels. A friend of Reba's was visiting from the States to stay with her for a few weeks. When she was leaving for the airport, he had snuck into the back of the bus and hid behind her luggage.

He had luckily escaped before anyone saw him and had stayed at the airport for three days until the police found him. He hadn't thought his escape plan through; he couldn't call his grandfather because he didn't have a number, nor could he call Maud, his only ally in Crimson Hills. He had been wholly unprepared.

Danger parked in the visitor's parking lot. Chex got out and stretched. "I am just going to find Maud. Say a quick hello, and then we will go home."

Maud was in the gift shop at the great house, lazily leafing through a picture book. The shop was empty.

"I thought you would have gone to Maurice Knight's funeral," Chex said at the door.

Maud looked up and widened her eyes. "Chex Knight!"

Chex nodded. He didn't bother correcting her that he hadn't used the name Knight since he was eighteen.

"Good Lord," Maud came around the counter and hugged him. "I can't even put my hands around you; you are so muscular, tall, and handsome. My goodness, you look really good, Chex. How are you?"

"I was fine until I came to Crimson Hills," Chex answered honestly.

Maud smiled, "I am so happy to see you nevertheless. Why didn't you go to the funeral?"

"I panicked," Chex said. "I was near there, but I couldn't do it."

"Even your voice is deeper," Maud grinned. "I imagine it

took a lot out of you to return here."

"It did," Chex said. "I had to come and say hello to you, though. I am heading back to Kingston now."

Maud smiled. "Okay, it was lovely seeing you again. When you come back to Crimson Hills, we'll have a proper catch-up."

Chex frowned. "I don't think I am ever coming back here, Maud."

Maud laughed. "Oh, you will."

Chex sighed. "Is this one of your predictions?"

Maud nodded. "Yes."

"I am going to defy it," Chex smiled.

"Oh, but you won't," Maud said. "I will see you soon."

For the first time, Maud would be wrong, Chex thought darkly. He was going to try his best to forget today at all costs.

He was good at compartmentalizing his thoughts. Today would be filed into the deepest recesses of his mental filing cabinet. He would forget he saw Garnet; he would forget he had a son, and he would pretend his father died twenty years ago and that today wasn't his funeral.

"Where to now, boss?" Danger looked at him when he sat in the car.

"Back to Kingston," Chex sighed.

Danger looked at him. He knew that expression on his boss's face; it meant that he wouldn't welcome conversation.

He drove out of the great house and back down the road; he slowed down when he saw Garnet's car leaving the house.

He turned to look at Chex to ask him if he should follow her, but Chex had his eyes closed.

Danger took it upon himself to follow her. He didn't know Crimson Hills, but his navigation worked. He wouldn't get lost, and besides, the place wasn't that big.

He drove slowly behind her. She was heading downhill as if she were leaving the community. Then they passed the church, and she put on her indicator. She was going to a place that said Crimson Hill Prep.

"She is probably going to pick up her son," Danger remarked.

"Why are we turning off?" Chex cracked one eye open.

"Because Garnet is turning, I decided to follow her."

"Oh," Chex said. He wasn't angry.

Danger breathed a sigh of relief.

****

They parked close to Garnet and watched as she hurriedly left the car. When she came back, her son was with her. She was hugging him around his shoulders, and he had his face pressed into her side as he hopped on one leg.

Chex inhaled audibly. He didn't know what he was feeling at the moment. His heart felt constricted like it could no longer beat. It felt like everything inside of him had tightened into a ball.

He watched as Garnet tousled Neon's hair and kissed him on the forehead. He was at the age where she could do so freely without protests. The connection between them was palpable; they had each other, they loved each other, and suddenly Chex wanted some of that, too.

They were his family. Whether he liked it or not. And honestly, he wasn't disliking it at all. In fact, he liked it a lot.

"He is a handsome little boy," Danger murmured. "What are you going to do?"

"I don't know," Chex murmured. "But I am going to do something."

Chapter Five

The family meeting was off to a good start. They had opted to meet by the poolside. Garwin, Erin, and Neon were playing ball in the water.

Gersham and Patti were conversing with someone on their phone at one end of the pool. Her Aunt Joy was strolling across the manicured lawn and staring around in disbelief.

As for her, she was painting her nails in an amber color, almost the same shade as Neon's eyes.

Chex's eyes.

She hadn't been able to get him out of her mind. Was that why she grabbed the amber-colored nail polish when she saw it at the pharmacy today while shopping for waterproof bandages for Neon's foot?

It was an unnecessary purchase; her collection had over twenty colors.

"I'm so proud of you for returning to school," Joy said, sitting beside her on a neighboring lounger. But I miss my little munchkin."

"I know, that's why you came to Crimson Hills," Garnet snickered, "you couldn't be away from Neon for long."

Joy chuckled. "I am guilty. Why didn't you finish up the degree in Kingston?"

"Because I just have a final project to do at the school in Montego Bay," Garnet replied. "That was what was standing between me and graduation, so I said, 'Why not?'"

"It's a great decision, and you need to spend some time with Neon alone," Joy said. "I am just being selfish."

"You and selfish can never be in the same sentence," Garnet said seriously. "You love us beyond reserve; you didn't bat an eyelid when I left Neon with you, and you have never asked me to do anything in return. You are the best aunt/mother/sister friend a person could have in their life, and let me say it out loud. I love and appreciate you, but I will not take you for granted a day more. You sacrificed your time and energy to raise me. It was unfair for me to give you my child to raise, too."

Joy brushed away tears from her eyes. "I love you too, kiddo."

And then she changed the subject. "I still can't believe what Leonard Crooks did to this place," Joy looked around. "He turned it into a resort."

"How was it when you lived here?" Garnet asked.

"It was one house," Joy said. "Four bedrooms upstairs, living room, family room, everything else downstairs. It seems as if he demolished the original house. Even the pool is different; we had a pool, but it wasn't as far back as this one, and it was not the size of this. And he dumped up the lawn area and took down the trees; when I lived here, the place was so heavily forested we couldn't see the sea from here."

"Who would have thought we had the same unfettered sea view as Crimson Hill Great House. It is gorgeous up here. How do you think Dad will take the changes?" Garnet asked.

"Quite well, I think," Joy said. "He sounded almost normal when I spoke to him last night. He sounds like the Sterling of old, the brother I used to know."

"I don't know the Sterling of old," Garnet said. "Such a pity."

"He was smart and charming, very close to our mother; he was a mama's boy. It's hard to imagine now, but back in the day, he was a sharp dresser," Joy chuckled, "he stepped up his game when he went for his MBA. When he came back, all the rich girls in the surrounding area wanted him. Mama found it all amusing."

And then she got married, inexplicably, to Leonard Crooks," Joy snorted. "He was just a twenty-one-year-old boy. Ma was sixty-two. She could have been his grandmother!"

Garnet chuckled. She never got tired of hearing her aunt rage over the same story.

"Maybe she just wanted her back blown out by a strapping young man," Garnet chuckled.

"I am no prude, I understand that, but to marry him," Fern shook her head, "everybody could see that he was up to no good. There was no talking my mom out of it; we begged and beseeched her not to marry Leonard. Sterling, her precious son, couldn't even stop her, and then a year later, poof, she was gone. Died mysteriously like all those girls Leonard Crooks had killed.

"I think that more than losing the house and the job, sent your father to drink; he just couldn't handle it. He blamed himself for her going through with it."

"Which is ridiculous," Garnet said. "Fern Silver had free will, and she chose the man over her children, her business, and common sense."

"He did something to my mother because I didn't recognize her after Leonard came into her life," Joy sighed. "I am looking forward to going to Leonard Crooks' sentencing hearing. I want to be there live; I want to see his face. I don't want to hear it from the news. I want the satisfaction of seeing that evil beast hauled off to jail. I hope they lock him away and throw away the key. I wonder if Sterling would want to go."

"I would want to go," Garnet said. "I was once friends with Madge Whitlock."

"Oh yes, DJ Duke's wife," Joy said, "the one who carried out the murders for Leonard."

"He was blackmailing her," Garnet protested.

"But she didn't have to do it," Joy pointed out. "I hope they lock her up and throw away the key, too."

"I have mixed feelings about that," Garnet said.

"You wouldn't if it were your family member she killed," Joy huffed. "She had a nice personality but was still a killer."

"Okay, Aunty," Garnet nodded, "you have a point."

Garwin emerged from the pool, leaving Erin and Neon. He flopped down in the other lounger beside Garnet. "Your son is so full of energy, and when I say full of energy, I mean he has more than is normal. And I do know how energetic little boys are; I teach them," Garwin chuckled.

"And that's why I am happy for the pool. When he goes in at night, he's out like a light by seven o'clock.

"I heard Chex was here yesterday," Garwin said. "Jack said he didn't attend his father's funeral."

"Uh huh," Garnet nodded.

"I also heard he came to our restaurant, had a conversation

with you, and left Marie a wad of money for a tip. She shared it with the other waitstaff and is still planning to buy a car."

"It wasn't that much money," Garnet chuckled. "Unless it's a toy car to give her grandson."

"Why are we talking about Chex?" Joy asked curiously. "Who is he?"

"The producer I used to work with a couple of years ago," Garnet said dismissively.

Garwin looked at her in shock. "So all this time, you haven't told Aunt Joy who Chex is?"

"No, it hasn't been important," Garnet mumbled. "I didn't tell anyone about Chex. You started rifling around in my business and jumped to conclusions."

"Chex is Maurice Knight's second son," Garwin said to Joy.

Joy frowned. "You know I've never met Maurice Knight, but I heard about him. He's popular around these parts for being strange. He didn't like leaving the farm."

"So that is why you didn't put two and two together. After all these years," Garwin murmured.

"What is he talking about?" Joy asked Garnet.

"Who knows what he is blathering about?" Garnet glared at Garwin.

"I got a program from yesterday. Gersham took it back after the repast. I skimmed through the pictures, and they were eye-opening. I took it to show Garnet."

Garwin went for the program and handed it to Joy first.

"Oh my," Joy looked at the front page and whistled. He was a handsome man, but this is not how I imagined he would look. They say the crazier they are, the better they appear."

Garnet chuckled.

"Does he look familiar?" Garwin prompted.

"Very," Joy frowned. "But I can't place who."

"Look at his baby pictures."

Joy skipped to the middle of the program and then looked at Garnet. "As I live and breathe, Neon is Maurice's twin."

Garnet sighed. "Maurice is his grandfather."

"Oh my," Joy said.

"That's all you're going to say?" Garwin asked. "After all these years."

"What are we talking about?" Gersham and Patti came over and pulled the chairs to form a circle.

"Garnet is doing the big reveal of who Neon's father is," Garwin said.

"Who is it?" Gersham asked. "Which one of the Knight brothers? Or is it Maurice Knight himself?"

"That's actually funny," Garnet chuckled. "I have never met Maurice Knight or any of Chex's brothers except Jack. Chex is Neon's father; we had a relationship for nearly two years that was equally passionate and maddening. I loved him and thought I could change him, but it didn't work out. The end."

"So why didn't you tell him about his son?" Joy asked. "I am confused. You said Neon's father was a mistake and you didn't want him involved. You said he would probably force you to have an abortion. I assumed he was a married man. Is Chex married?"

"No," Garnet snorted. "Chex has never wanted children, and he was quite vocal about it. I got pregnant when we were on a break; I wasn't taking any contraception at the time… It's a long story... but here we are."

"So, does he know about Neon now?" Patti asked.

"More or less," Garnet shrugged. "I told him that Neon was mine. He didn't ask many questions; he was a bit overwhelmed. It was his father's funeral, and he couldn't even bring himself to go. Finding out he was a father when he expressly said he didn't want to pass on any of his father's genes to any child was a bit too much for him at the moment."

"But why doesn't he want children?" Joy asked, flabbergasted. "I don't get it."

"His father tortured him," Garnet said. "It wasn't only physical abuse; Maurice Knight took religious fanaticism to another level. He used to have Chex fasting for his sins, punished him for all sorts of infractions, and locked him away in the dark. It was bad."

"But why?" Joy still looked confused.

"Because God was going to come at any moment, and they had to be pure," Garnet said. "And every so often, Maurice would get visions about God's impending coming and pull them out of school and have them cleansing themselves from impure thoughts and whatnot."

"I've heard some of the stories from Jack," Garwin murmured.

"And we thought we had it bad with our drunken father," Gersham said. "There is always someone better or worse off, isn't there?"

"True," Patti nodded.

"I remember a little bit about Maurice Knight," Joy said. "Apart from the rumors that he had some screws loose and he was building his own community up in the hills waiting for the end of times. I remember when they were going strong. One of the men, I can't remember his name now, wanted Maurice's wife. What's her name?"

"Laurel," Garwin answered.

"Yes, one of the men wanted Laurel to be his wife," Joy continued. "And Maurice was like, 'No, no, I'm not having some sister-wife situation up here.' And the guy was like,

'But we had sister-wife situations in the Bible.' And there was a big hullabaloo. And the next thing I know, they disbanded."

"So how is it you never met Maurice?" Gersham asked.

"He didn't leave the farm, and I've only ever been to the farm shop," Joy said. By the time Maurice came to Crimson Hills and sequestered himself on the farm, I was married and lived in Kingston. When I came back to take care of you children, the cult was up and running, and he didn't leave the place. I can't recall seeing him walking, driving, or doing anything on the road. He certainly never ate at our cook shop."

"I don't think he has ever left the farm. except when he was sick, they took him to the hospital," Garwin said. "I think he may have had that thing where people don't like to leave a space they find familiar."

Joy nodded. "So my nephew is a Knight. Neon Knight, oh my goodness, that's his middle name! I remember seeing it on the birth certificate and thinking, Garnet broke the tradition of no middle names in the family."

Garwin and Gersham looked at each other.

"How did we not know that?" Garwin asked. "I didn't know my nephew's middle name. I probably would have put two and two together long before this if I had known you named him Knight."

Garnet laughed. "It's not a big deal. Besides, Chex is not a Knight. He is a Hastings. He legally changed his name to his grandfather's when he turned eighteen."

"So, is Chex going to be in Neon's life?" Gersham asked.

"I doubt it," Garnet said.

"Maybe it's for the best," Joy said. "I hope he's not as cuckoo as his father because if that is the case, we don't need him. Neon is quite fine with just us."

Erin and Neon came out of the pool. Erin dried off Neon and hugged him with the towel. "I didn't know you guys started the family meeting."

"We haven't," Garnet said. "We were just discussing the pictures in Maurice Knight's funeral program and how a certain someone looks just like him."

"Ah," Erin nodded. She couldn't say anything more; Neon was heading for Garnet, and he sat on her lap.

Garnet hugged him to her. "Are you hungry, sweetheart?"

"Not yet," Neon said. "Can we go back in the pool?"

"Tomorrow," Garnet kissed him on his forehead.

She looked at her family. "I will need to see to his shower and give him a snack soon."

"So we'll make this quick," Gersham said, "Dad will be out of rehab next week. Aunt Joy is going for him; she'll take him back here, and we'll have a gathering. Garnet suggested we keep it simple, just us as a family. Any objections?"

"None," everybody said.

"Patti and I are in talks to sell Rafferty House back to Crimson Hill Great House Estate. They made an offer just now, and we accepted."

"Oh, cool," Garnet said.

"Congrats," Garwin said.

"It is a nice house," Erin said, "And I didn't encounter one ghost when I lived there."

Patti chuckled. "What can I say? I see into other dimensions."

Gersham said, "The next item on the agenda is Silver Chemicals. Aunt Joy will tell us more about that."

"Yes," Joy said, "Sterling and I discussed it; we are willing to sell it. I don't have any interest, and he is definitely not interested."

"There is a company, Flamenco Chemicals, who is

begging to merge it with theirs," Gersham said. The lawyers said the price is good, so that could happen shortly; Aunt Joy will be the point person on that. She will be acting on behalf of Dad."

Joy nodded. "The proceeds of the sale will be split among us equally, so that's something to look forward to."

Garnet nodded. "Blessings upon blessings, we deserve it."

"That's not all," Joy said, "Sterling is adamant that we put a restrictive covenant on this property, like the one on our grandparents' place. This property cannot be sold to outsiders; ownership should always rest with a Silver family blood relative. The five of us will be on the title, and only your children will be able to inherit."

"Makes sense," Garwin said.

"The lawyers will be sending over the paperwork by the end of the week," Joy said.

"So you didn't come here just to check up on me," Garnet chuckled.

"Nope," Joy smiled, "I came to sort out our family business."

"Is this the conclusion of our family meeting?" Garnet asked. "I need to ensure this guy showers and gets something to eat."

"Yes, it is," Gersham said.

"Everything is falling into place nicely," Joy said wistfully, "my nephews are happily married, but my niece…"

"Don't you start," Garnet said, "I am just fine."

Chapter Six

Was she really ok? Garnet made a cup of chamomile and went to sit on her balcony. The place was still; you could hear a pin drop. It was after twelve o'clock, but her mind was too keyed up to settle.

How had she ended up here? On this trajectory?

She had it all figured out; she would work the hotel circuit and then try to break into the music business. She should have made it big by twenty-five, hearing her music on the airwaves everywhere. And then, with that accomplished, she would move into the production side of things; that was what fascinated her.

She remembered when she had shared her plans with Chex; he had nodded solemnly, "That sounds like a good plan," he had said. They had been in the studio for most of the night, working on one particular song for DJ Duke's album.

She had learned since working with Chex that he didn't

sleep at night, and he expected that no one would sleep too while working on a project. He was professional with everyone and had no problems keeping her at arm's length, even though she was sure he could sense that she liked him. For a brief time, she had started wearing more shape-accentuating clothes, but that had only attracted the attention of the other guys. Not Chex.

Chex did not find her appealing at all. In a desperate effort to make him notice her, she had accepted a dinner date with Sam, the manager, in front of him. Chex had only commented, "You do know he is old enough to be your father?"

"Age is just a number," she had said flippantly. What was forty-five to her twenty?

Unfortunately, the date did not go well. Sam was too handsy for her. He had expected her to sleep with him after dinner, and he only talked about himself.

"How was the date last night?" Chex asked when he saw her again the next evening.

"Not good," Garnet said, "What's wrong with modern men? Doesn't anyone understand the concept of getting to know someone before you jump into bed with them?"

Chex laughed. "People are short on time; they just want to jump to the good stuff. If the main reason why you are seeing someone is sex, why beat around the bush when you know that's what all the dates are for? Get the sex out of the way and then move on from there."

"That's doing things backward," Garnet said. "You become friends, then you have sex. You get married, then you have children. Any other way is asking for trouble."

Chex looked at her contemplatively. "I don't have sex with my female friends. Once they are in the friend zone, that's it. I don't cross lines; you are either a friend or lover."

Garnet swallowed. "Okay."

"I don't make promises either," Chex said, "Marriage and children are a solid no for me."

Garnet nodded. "Fair enough."

Chex smiled. "I also don't date people who work for me. I will not be a cliché, the producer sleeping with his artist."

"But I'm just a backup singer. I'm not your artist," Garnet protested, not realizing she had revealed how she felt about him.

But Chex saw it. He looked at her intently and then shook his head, "You just turned twenty, fresh out of your teens; you are in your second year in college. You are a good girl, an idealist. You have a crush.

"It's normal to think you have feelings for me. You actually don't; you'll get over it. I am ten years older than you are; I've been there and done that, and I am jaded and damaged.

"Trust me when I tell you this, Garnet. You will be thankful that I am leaving you alone to grow up. Make your mistakes with other people, explore, and have adventures. Don't be caught up in feelings and commitment."

"So you wouldn't have a problem if I slept with all the guys in the building?" Garnet asked.

Chex laughed, "I'd tell you to protect yourself."

"I forgot that you wouldn't have a problem with that. I heard you only sleep with sex workers or very experienced women," Garnet smirked.

"Sex workers need love too," Chex said.

"So what," Garnet whispered, "are we going to be just friends?"

"I am not sure," Chex said. "I am quite comfortable not labeling us at the moment."

He then changed the subject abruptly. "Tell me about your ambitions to be a music composer? Have you created any beats for yourself?"

"Yes, of course," Garnet nodded. "That's how I got my music scholarship. I created a portfolio of original compositions and submitted it as part of the application process."

"Oh, cool," Chex nodded.

"I've always been passionate about expressing myself through music in whatever way I can, and composing allows me to do that. I want to evoke emotions and tell stories through my compositions, whether for films, video games, or standalone pieces."

"So, what genre are you interested in?" Chex asked.

"I love mixing it up," Garnet said. "I've created beats and musical pieces that range from classical to contemporary."

"I'd like to hear some of your work," Chex said. "I have a project I'm working on; I wouldn't mind a second opinion. If we work well together, I can see us doing some collabs."

****

Garnet found out they worked well together. Creatively, they were in sync. It didn't go unnoticed by either of them that they had a vibe. They finished the project that was giving Chex trouble, and she did most of the composing. It was fun, and he was pleased with the result.

She had stopped trying to attract Chex; he was indifferent to her on a personal level, and she didn't want any of the guys around to treat her differently, either. So, she gave herself a buzz-cut Sinead O'Connor style and continued wearing her baggy clothes. After a while, they seemed to forget she was a girl, especially when she wore her baseball cap.

"You could have told us you were a lesbian," Phil, one of the engineers who had initially pursued her, said. "We don't judge around here."

Chex overheard their conversation and found it hilarious.

"Have you ever had a boyfriend?" Chex asked her when they were packing up to leave one night. They were winding down the project, an infomercial for a development company.

"Never," Garnet said. "I am as pure as the undriven snow."

"I wonder why," Chex mused. "You do know the buzz cut and the baggy clothes are not a deterrent if someone is serious about you. You are still pretty, and you have a nice body."

"Thanks, I guess," Garnet said sleepily.

"And you are quirky, funny, and special," Chex mused. "I actually like you."

"I guess that means we are friends now?" Garnet grinned.

"No," Chex shook his head. "I am still unwilling to put you in the friend zone."

He turned off the lights, and she brushed past him into the passageway. He grabbed her hand and pulled her closer.

"I don't know if I am ready for this," Garnet swallowed nervously.

"Okay," Chex said. "Then tell me to leave you alone." He ran his fingers along her arm, and she tingled all the way to her toes.

"I don't want to tell you that," Garnet said.

Chex sighed and stepped away. "You don't know what's bad for you."

"And you don't know what's good for you," Garnet retorted.

Chex laughed. "Touché."

They entered the lobby; it was raining heavily. There were people up and about.

"Visibility is zero; I am going back to the office. I might

as well get some work done," Traci from advertising passed them.

"Maybe we should go to my office and wait this out," Chex said.

Chex's office was large and modern, with expansive windows overlooking the cityscape. However, the view was obscured because of the rain. It was coming down in sheets. A huge desk was the room's focal point, with a large leather chair behind it, and several comfortable chairs were arranged before it. Garnet sat in one and looked around. There was a long L-shaped settee along one wall. The walls were adorned with framed platinum records, showcasing Chex's successful collaborations and hit releases. There were also colorful and vibrant artworks reminiscent of album cover designs.

"The art is cute," Garnet murmured.

"Thanks, I did them myself," Chex said as he sat beside her. They were both facing his chair.

"You did?" Garnet widened her eyes. "Are you serious? Is there anything you can't do in the creative sphere?"

"I haven't tried to play the trombone. I've taught myself everything else," Chex chuckled. "Would you like a drink?"

"No, thanks. I don't drink, and it's two o'clock in the morning," Garnet grimaced. "I don't know how you do it."

"Do what?" Chex asked.

"Seem so alert in the night," Garnet answered. "I feel very sleepy as soon as it hits eleven o'clock. My foot starts to twitch, and my body starts getting heavy." She yawned. "You must have chronic insomnia."

"Actually, I have no problems sleeping," Chex said. I prefer to do it during the day. I go to bed around six in the morning and then wake up around two. That's eight hours. That's quite in keeping with the recommended daily sleep recommendation."

"But why are you like that?" Garnet asked.

"A holdover from my childhood," Chex sighed. "Being locked in a place with no windows and in complete darkness for hours. Like solitary confinement in prison."

"Who did that to you?" Garnet gasped.

"My dad," Chex looked at her. "We lived in a place called Crimson Hills."

"That's where I am from," Garnet said.

"Now, this is getting interesting," Chex murmured.

"My dad killed my mom," Garnet said. "And went to prison for it."

"Ah, I heard about that. That's your family?" Chex murmured.

"Yup," Garnet nodded.

"So what was it like growing up with that burden?" Chex asked.

"I had my aunt and brothers. I was too young to really process what happened. I don't remember much about those early days. I was five years old," Garnet explained.

"Oh," Chex nodded. "It's good that you weren't traumatized by it. How is your relationship with your dad now?"

"Non-existent," Garnet shrugged.

"Mine too," Chex nodded. "I am on the brink of suggesting we be friends; we have so many things in common, bad fathers being one." Chex laced his fingers with hers. "But I am not going to. The more we talk, the more I don't want to be your friend."

"That's fine, Chex. Anything you say," Garnet rested her head on his shoulder. She could barely keep her eyes open.

The next thing she knew, she was waking up on Chex's sofa. He had moved her to his couch and covered her with a blanket. There was a note under her phone.

I didn't want to disturb you; you were sleeping so peacefully. I went to my apartment. I would have taken you with me, but it isn't a good idea. You said you are not sure you want this, and I respect that. See you later. Chex.

Why had she said that? She felt like kicking herself all day.

Chapter Seven

DJ Duke's album launch was near the end of the summer at the studio concert hall. Garnet attended as one of the backup singers; they would perform live. Most of the music fraternity was there to support DJ Duke, creating a convivial atmosphere. She wore snug-fitting black pants and a white peasant top.

When she got there, Chex was nowhere in sight. She had hoped she would spot him and indulge in some of the witty banter they usually shared. This was the last time she would see him before school. The summer had flown by so fast.

"So, what's next for you?" Madge, DJ Duke's wife, asked her. They were sitting in the performing area at the back. Madge, as usual, was there to support her husband. She gave him a pep talk before every performance. Garnet found them to be sweet.

"Third year of college," Garnet said.

"You should grow out your hair," Madge said, "and dress

up some more."

Garnet grinned. "I feel comfortable the way I am."

"But if you like Chex," Madge whispered, "you have to do something. Spruce up yourself a little more."

"Didn't you hear? I am a lesbian," Garnet whispered back.

Madge chuckled. "I don't believe that for a second. I see the way you look at Chex."

Chex walked into the room at the same time, with a woman clinging to his arms.

"Uh oh," Madge said, "Keira Mendez, condom model. She runs an OnlyFans account, too, where she does stuff with vegetables."

"What, she eats them? People pay to see that?" Garnet asked incredulously.

Madge laughed. "How are you so innocent?"

Garnet inhaled. Keira was everything she was not, dressed to the hilt in a body-hugging dress that barely covered her thighs, a pound of makeup, hair that reached her butt, and eyelashes that could double as fly swats.

"So, that's Chex's type," Garnet noted.

Her eyes collided with his as he talked to DJ Duke. Keira was clinging to his side like glue. Garnet dragged her eyes away from his.

"So, is that his girlfriend?" she asked Madge.

Madge was on her phone. She looked up at Garnet. "Who are we talking about? Chex doesn't have girlfriends. He has bed partners. I thought you knew the score."

Garnet swallowed. "Apparently, I didn't."

"Oh, girl," Madge said, "you didn't fall for him, did you?"

"No, I didn't," Garnet protested.

"Good," Madge looked at her doubtfully, "because you would get hurt. After this, you'll return to school and find a nice boy to date. Chex is not a nice boy. He is a wolf; he eats nice girls like you for breakfast."

She left the album launch after she performed. She didn't want to stay a moment longer.

"Why are you leaving so early?" Chex asked her before she could enter her car. She didn't even know he had followed her.

"I am tired," Garnet said. "I have to go home and do some prepping for school. I return on Monday."

"I see," Chex nodded.

They stared at each other, not speaking for a long while. Garnet didn't know what to say. Should she thank him for the opportunity? Should she thank him for resisting her all summer and keeping her at arm's length? Or should she express her hurt, questioning why he hadn't pursued her and potentially broken her heart? She felt like a mess.

"Well, okay then," she exhaled, realizing she had been holding her breath until now.

"I'll call you," Chex said.

She nodded jerkily, not expecting him to follow through.

As he turned to leave, he looked back. "Which song would you inject here if our lives were a movie?"

"Really?" Garnet grinned.

"Humor me."

"For Just A Moment, by David Foster," Garnet said, "just the instruments. You walk away, and the chorus plays: 'Time goes on, people touch, and then they're gone…' I get into my car and cry dramatically. You go back to the party with Keira Mendez, who does stuff with vegetables, kissing her passionately while I cry my eyes out. The end."

Chex laughed heartily. "Keira is a friend. And you know my rules about friends and lovers. I really will keep in touch with you; I meant that.

"I like your song selection, but I would change it to Love

From a Distance by Beres Hammond. I would also change the scenario; the focus would be on me, I watch you wistfully as you go into your car, and I'll stand here like a sad figure while Beres sings. *I see love from a distance coming but slowly, I know it's gonna last forever, I feel us coming closer, closer and closer.*

"You go back into your car smiling, knowing that I like you and that you have me wrapped around those dainty little fingers of yours, and I go back to the party thinking about you, finding no joy in it because you are gone, and then I go home alone. All the while fighting my feelings, wondering why I didn't take it further in the summer and yet happy that I didn't because you are special," Chex added. "In my scenario, I am the sad one, and you leave happy knowing I am conflicted where you are concerned."

"Oh, Chex," Garnet whispered. "I don't know what to say."

"Listen out for a call." Chex said, "I might even call you tonight, I miss you already."

She still went into her car and cried tears of relief. He had just admitted that he had feelings for her; she was not alone in this.

****

No Promises was the hottest song for the fall. Everybody was singing the chorus.

In the city lights where shadows dance, whispers in the wind taking a chance. Walking down the street, lost in reverie. No Promises tonight, just you and me.

When the duet remix came out, she became a mini-celebrity at her school.

"You gained invaluable practical experience this summer, Garnet," Mr. Hudson, her Professional Development and

Portfolio Building teacher, had said to her. What you learned on the job from Right Vibes Production House is invaluable. Basically, you are doing what this course is about building a professional portfolio, networking in the industry, and preparing for a career in music and film with one of the hottest producers in the business right now."

And then, quite unexpectedly, Chex showed up at her school with his imposing-looking bodyguard and driver, Danger. He had called her as he had promised every day. They chatted about everything. They even wrote songs together. He hadn't told her that he would show up, though.

"Excuse me, Miss, where's a nice place to eat around here?" he asked when he saw her heading for the parking lot.

Garnet smiled. She hadn't stopped crushing on him one bit. The feelings were still there, stronger, brighter. She felt like falling on him like an eager puppy in pure, unadulterated happiness.

"My granduncle Rufus is playing at the Beach Hut this Wednesday," Garnet said. "Their food is decent, and the band is above average."

"Okay," Chex grinned.

"So, what have you been up to?" Chex asked casually after they ordered their food. They had both ordered the chef's special.

"Nothing much, the usual. School, work, construction," Garnet shrugged. "I didn't know you were coming this way. I would have dressed up."

"Garnet!" Mr. Hudson intruded before Chex could respond.

Garnet smiled at her teacher. He looked between her and Chex and waited expectantly.

"Oh," Garnet grinned. "Mr. Hudson, this is Chex Hastings.

Chex, this is Mr. Hudson."

"You should come by for Career Day," Mr. Hudson said to Chex. "We would be honored to have a multitalented person like you darken our doors."

"I'll see if I am free," Chex said, handing him a business card. Mr. Hudson walked away happily.

"You like older guys, don't you?" Chex asked when Mr. Hudson was out of earshot.

"He is my teacher," Garnet laughed. "I don't even know his first name."

"He was looking at you with a little adoration in his gaze," Chex said. "I don't like it."

Garnet's ears perked up. She stared at Chex in awe. "You sound jealous."

Chex laughed. "I don't do jealous. What are you doing this Christmas holiday?"

"I'm working," Garnet said. "I am booked all through the holidays. I don't think I will be sleeping."

Chex smiled. "I like your work ethic. You are always booked and busy."

"I have to be. I am currently building a place with my brother. I have to pull my weight. Why did you ask about Christmas?"

"I am throwing a party at my house in Stony Hill. It's on Christmas Eve. I'll put you on the invite list. Bring a plus one."

That was the thing about Chex. He would make her feel special by telling her he didn't like how someone looked at her and then deflate her with an offhand invitation to bring a plus one. But her feelings about Chex aside, when he threw a party, it was an industry party. Everyone who is anyone in the music business would be there.

She had heard on the grapevine that his Stony Hills house

was magnificent. She wanted to see it. She would cancel her gig for Christmas Eve and Christmas Day just so she could attend.

"I'll see how it goes," she said nonchalantly.

"No," Chex said, "you'll show up. I am looking forward to seeing you in a dress."

****

The Stony Hill mansion was indeed impressive. She had no problems finding the place. It stood alone in a cul-de-sac on a sparsely populated hill with houses resembling hotels.

She had to hand in her invitation to security guard at the front before she was waved through.

Arlene was her plus one; she had practically begged Garnet to take her. "You owe me," Arlene said. "You got chosen for DJ Duke's album, and I wasn't."

Garnet hadn't bothered arguing with her weird logic. She was one of six people who did backup on different songs.

She had taken Arlene because she didn't want to go alone. Chex had said she should carry a plus one, and it would be pathetic not to have one.

When Garnet picked her up, Arlene was dressed to the hilt. She wore a silver mini dress that looked like it had been poured on her, with cutouts all over at strategic places. She wore a long ponytail wig and bright silver eyeshadow that glittered whenever she blinked.

"Oh wow," Garnet had whistled. "You came to slay."

"Thanks," Arlene grinned. "What are you in?"

"A dress," Garnet said.

"It's nice," Arlene murmured, "but it screams Sunday School, not the hottest party of the year."

"Stony Hill is cold. My weather app said the low tonight would be 17 degrees Celsius. My poor tropical heart can't stand it," Garnet said. "I am not going to go there and be uncomfortable. The party is outside, and there is wind."

Arlene frowned and looked her over. "You have a point, but a turtleneck, though? Why not show a bit of skin somewhere?"

Garnet had dressed practically in a figure-hugging red turtleneck sweater dress with long sleeves that flared at the end. It outlined her shape but wasn't too tight, hitting just at her knee. She had paired it with minimal makeup and red strawberry-flavored lip gloss to match her dress, which would have to be replenished throughout the night because she kept licking it off—it tasted good. She had finished the look with large hoop earrings she borrowed from her aunt.

She had never been comfortable with anything too tight or too short. Her aunt Joy was responsible for that.

"You are a pretty girl," her aunt gave her the speech when she was twelve, "you can't help that. Boys are going to flock to you like bees to honey; women are going to envy you. It won't be easy. People will not see your wonderful personality. You will be judged. But remember, my dear, your beauty is just one facet of who you are. True beauty radiates from within. A pretty face may catch someone's eye, but a beautiful soul captures hearts. You, my sweet niece, will be beautiful inside and out."

Garnet had chosen clothing that reflected her comfort and style rather than conforming to societal expectations since then. She had preferred to cover up and cut her hair because she embraced the challenge of breaking free from the expectations placed on her appearance.

And through the years, it had given her a certain thrill to hear people say, "If I had your hair, skin, or shape, I would do so much more with it."

She didn't mind Arlene calling her a Sunday School teacher. She was almost sure that she would be the most modestly dressed person at the party, but at least she would be warm and could have cold drinks. Arlene was visibly shuddering when they stepped out of the parking lot.

Garnet grinned. "Can't say I didn't warn you."

"I am going to have to dance all night to stay warm," Arlene complained.

Garnet chuckled. "No thanks, I get my cardio in every night while performing. Tonight, I will chill, eat the food, meet the people, and have fun."

"My lips are vibrating," Arlene grumbled. "It's cold."

She was still chuckling at Arlene when they approached the party area, which had an infinity pool and a panoramic view of the city.

"Oh, wow," Garnet said as they approached the rear of the house. "It's fantastic."

The party was just getting started. It was eleven o'clock on Christmas Eve, and mellow music played in the background. Quite a few people were already there, including a haze of local celebrities. DJ Duke and Madge stopped her first, and they chit-chatted a little. She knew when Chex came behind her. She was aware of him before he even spoke.

"Hey," he said. "You look gorgeous as usual."

Garnet smiled. "So do you." He was dressed in his usual black, but he wore a jacket this time. His inside shirt was obviously silk. A few buttons were opened at the top, showing the column of his throat. She could see his necklace—a big 'C.'

And he smelled heavenly. His perfume had to be custom-made; nobody smelled like Chex.

"I have something for you."

"You-you-you-do?" Garnet stuttered.

"Uh, yes," Chex nodded. "Come with me."

He led her to a guest house with its own pool and handed her a small square gift-wrapped box.

"Oh wow, I didn't get you anything," Garnet murmured.

"That's quite fine," Chex said. "Open it."

She did. Inside was a silver necklace with a red heart-shaped stone.

"It's gorgeous," she breathed.

"It's a garnet stone in a silver setting," Chex said, "a garnet in silver for Garnet Silver. It sounds corny when I say it out loud. Here, let me put it on."

He did and then stood back.

"This is thoughtful," Garnet whispered. "Thank you."

"I bought it a couple of months ago," Chex said. "I was waiting for the right time to give it to you. Let's go have some fun." He moved toward the door.

"What does this mean?" Garnet asked.

"It means that I like you," Chex said, "a lot."

"But I am still not your friend," Garnet said, stepping out of the house.

"No," Chex said, "definitely not."

****

They spoke almost every day in the new year. They even collaborated on a beat that became popular.

Then, Chex called her on February first. "Happy Birthday."

Garnet smiled; he remembered the conversation when she said she celebrated her birthday all month, especially when it wasn't a leap year.

"I am staying in Montego Bay," he said. "We can celebrate

all month. Tonight, I have a party at Club Meds; you can be my date."

"I have school," Garnet protested.

"Then come and stay with me for the month. Your school is nearby."

"I can't," Garnet said.

"It's a big villa," Chex said, "you have your own room. I won't touch you if that's what you want."

"What if I want you to touch me?" Garnet asked.

"Then you head to the doctor for contraception after school today," Chex said. "I'll give you directions to the villa from there."

She went to the doctor, opted to get her shots, and drove to the villa. It was a Half-Moon property, luxurious as expected, with seven bedrooms and a stunning sea view.

"We'll have people joining us next week," Chex said after showing her around. "But they don't have to get in our way. You can take the room next to mine."

Garnet nodded. She was nervous. This was a new step for her, for them.

"We don't have to change our status," Chex said to her earnestly. "We can continue as we are."

"So you'll keep me as not a friend, not a lover, and then I dangle here in no man's land, still a virgin at twenty-one?"

Chex cupped her cheek. "You look so edible."

Garnet laughed.

"I think when we finally become intimate, you are going to break me," Chex said. "No, I don't think it, I know. This is going to mean something. You are different."

Garnet smiled. That was music to her ears.

"I don't think you realize what I am saying here, Garnet," Chex looked at her. "I think I inherited what my father had, call it a madness. He could become fixated and obsessed with things, people, and events. I don't want to become obsessed with you."

"We'll try not to," Garnet said, reaching up and putting her lips squarely on his.

That first kiss, by the balcony overlooking the sea, was electrifying.

She skipped school a lot that February. Every night, they went out to a different event, and every night, they made love. Then, they stayed up in the wee hours talking about everything and nothing.

She tried not to think about an inevitable goodbye. She thought that Chex would return to Kingston after February, but he stayed. He rented another villa for the long term. March melted into April and then May. They spent most of their weekends together. It was like a honeymoon without the marriage; he treated her as if he loved her without saying a word, and she didn't want to jinx what they had.

It was perfect. She thought everything was going well. Chex treated her as if she were his whole world.

In the summer, he arranged for her to tour with DJ Duke. She liked to think it was because he didn't want them apart; he didn't even pretend that he wanted her in another room. She stayed with Chex wherever they went. Everyone knew she was Chex's girl. Even Madge remarked to her one night before she performed with DJ Duke.

"Girl, I don't know what you did to Chex, but you have him whipped. I have never seen someone so into a woman. It makes me jealous. Duke loves me, but not with that possessive edge. It's like the man needs you to breathe."

Chex overheard Madge, and somehow, it was never the same after that. He started withdrawing from her, little by little. By the end of summer, he told her that it was over. Garnet had felt as if her whole world was crashing around her.

"I didn't make you any promises, Garnet," he stated. She nodded stiffly.

"I think we should both move on."

"Why?" she asked, feeling a little shell-shocked. "Is it what Madge said? Isn't it? She pointed out that you had some emotions toward me, and that's it—you are calling it quits on us."

Chex stared at her stonily. "I must do this, or I'll hurt you in the long run."

"I am not begging you to be with me," Garnet growled. "If it's over, it's over. Goodbye. I'll move on."

****

"Mommy," Neon came into her room looking for her.

"I am here, sweetie." Garnet closed the patio door and joined Neon in the bed. She smoothed back his curls and kissed him on the forehead. "Go back to sleep," she said.

He was out in no time. Her cheeks were wet. She had been silently crying. She wiped her face, closed her eyes, and saw Chex's face behind her eyelids. She hadn't moved on from him and yesterday had brought it all back.

Chapter Eight

"**W**hy haven't I seen you for the past few days?" Philip frowned when Chex walked into the kitchen in the morning. "And you don't answer your phone anymore? I needed proof of life. I seriously considered reporting you missing when I called Danger, and he said you were fine."

"I was at my Kingston apartment; I'm going through some things."

"What things?" Philip frowned. "I thought you had a therapist?"

"I fired him," Chex shrugged, "he suggested that I attend the funeral."

"Ah," Philip nodded.

"I made it as far as Crimson Hills," Chex said, "But I just couldn't go farther."

"You can't blame him for that. You were doing so well with therapy; you quit smoking and drinking."

"I had a relapse," Chex sighed, "I spent all weekend high.

I was trying to suppress my emotions, but it didn't work. The only thing I ended up with was a raging headache, some hallucinations, and a certainty that something is seriously wrong with me."

"You have always been hard on yourself," Philip said, "be kinder, rehire your therapist."

"Remember when I told you that I met a girl at a nightclub, caught feelings, and she stole from me?"

Philip nodded.

"It was a lie," Chex sighed. "I had to tell you something to cover up my bad mood at the time and my bitterness against women. I met someone, fought my feelings for her for close to a year, and then broke up with her when I realized that I was in too deep. I didn't even recognize myself in the mirror anymore.

"I was turning into an obsessed stalker; I watched her at school, I constantly checked her social media profiles, and questioned her every move. It wasn't healthy, and I knew I had to break free from that toxic cycle. I was turning into Dad."

Philip looked stunned. "You were doing all of that? Who was this girl?"

"Garnet Silver," Chex said. "She wasn't a stripper, a call girl, an exotic dancer, or one of the usual girls I hung around with. She was sweet and pure, and I didn't want to ruin her, but I pursued her anyway.

"And then, when I started acting like Dad, I made the difficult decision to end the relationship, even though it felt like tearing a part of myself away. The aftermath was tough. I tried to lose myself in the party life. I told myself it didn't matter what I felt, and she didn't matter.

"I deliberately didn't check to see what was going on with her because I knew if she was seeing someone else or had truly moved on, I couldn't handle it."

Philip nodded. "I understand that."

"Because I was determined to cut her out of my life," Chex said. "I didn't know she was pregnant and that she had my baby. And now he is a boy of five. I have a kid."

"What?" Philip was in the process of reaching for a mug to pour his coffee, his hand stilled.

Chex clasped his head in his hands. "You heard me."

"I know the name, Silver," Philip mused. "Where have I heard that before?"

"From Crimson Hills," Chex murmured.

"Oh yes," Philip nodded. "Sterling Silver. His mother, Fern Silver, died mysteriously after marrying Leonard Crooks and left everything to him in her will. It nearly destroyed Sterling. He went from rich to dirt poor in a matter of months. And then he turned into a drunkard and killed his girlfriend, Tina Boyd. I saw her once; she was quite pretty."

"Apparently," Chex said, "Sterling didn't actually kill Tina; it was probably an accident. According to my detective report…"

Philip raised an eyebrow and took a sip of his coffee.

"I had a report commissioned to discover everything I could on Garnet."

"Oh," Philip said.

"Her mother's real name was Anya Chan. It's a long story."

"I think I know the story," Philip said. "I read it in the paper. It caught my eye because it was about Crimson Hills, and we do business with Samir Chan; he's a client of ours at Hastings Hardware. They use us for their major construction projects."

"Yep," Chex nodded.

"So, what else did you learn about Garnet Silver?" Philip asked.

"She had Neon, left him with her aunt, and worked on a cruise ship for two years. She has always been financially independent. I doubt Neon needs anything materially."

"That's the name of the boy?"

"Yes," Chex nodded.

"Interesting name," Philip nodded.

"His full name is interesting; she named him Neon Knight Silver. She used our original surname for a middle name, like a little nod to his heritage."

"Love it," Philip grinned. "Pearl and I were thinking of double-barreling our baby's name when we have one, Knight-Hastings."

"You'll love his picture even more," Chex said, pulling his phone from his pocket. "This is your nephew."

"Oh my, he is a Knight, all right," Philip looked at the picture. "He looks like me, with your eyes. When can we meet him?"

"I am working on it," Chex sighed. "I can't just go charging into Garnet's life. I don't think she would let me. She emphasized that he was hers. I guess just in case I got any ideas."

"You have a right to be in Neon's life," Philip said. "He is your son, too. A boy needs his father."

"I did not need mine," Chex said. "I would have done wonderfully without him."

"True," Philip murmured, "but it's because of Dad that you, me, Jack will be better fathers than he ever was. You, in particular, will be a stellar dad."

"I don't know about that," Chex shook his head. "I never wanted children. It has not even crossed my mind. I did a vasectomy to prevent this, remember?"

"Yes, that vasectomy that I told you not to do. And yet here you are, with a child. This is fascinating."

Philip picked up the picture again.

"What's so fascinating?" Pearl walked into the kitchen.

Chex sighed. Pearl was about to make a big deal out of this. She and Philip had been married for nearly eighteen months, and they were trying to have a baby. She had baby on the brain, and Neon's resemblance to Phillip would set her off.

"Oh my God," Pearl took the phone from Philip. "You have a son? Why am I just learning about this?"

Philip chuckled and kissed her, "You know I don't hide anything from you, babe. This is Chex's son."

"He's extremely cute," Pearl breathed.

"Of course, you would think so; he looks just like Phillip," Chex smirked. "He is your dream child."

"That's true, I can't argue with that," Pearl said, "What's his name? Who is his mom? When can we meet him?"

"His name is Neon, and his mother's name is Garnet. I am trying to figure out when I can meet him again. He is in Crimson Hills for the summer with his mom. She sends him to a fancy summer school there while she returns to school to finish her degree."

"Ah," Pearl smiled, "so she is not one of your regular women."

"No," Chex sighed, "she was different."

"Why was she different?" Pearl asked.

"Feelings got involved," Chex said, "from the moment I met her, I knew it would get messy. I tried to avoid her, but it didn't work out. And here we are."

"Here we are," Pearl mused. "What's the strategy to get back your family?"

Chex stared at Pearl in shock. The way she said 'family' just felt right. But he wasn't going to be sucked into that line of thought. He didn't dare dream about normal. He wasn't normal. He had almost locked Garnet up and thrown away the key. She didn't know how close he had come to being unhinged by her. Maybe there was some way for him to have a role in Neon's life without contact with Garnet. Just the brief encounter with her a week ago had him in a tizzy; it's as if the last five years didn't happen. All his attempts to purge her out of his system had been for naught.

"I think you should stay at the farm for the summer," Philip said. "That way, you would be close to Neon."

"Hell no," Chex shook his head.

"Dad is not there anymore; Knightsbridge is a harmless place; the mad king is gone," Philip urged. "Mom is planning to renovate the house. And Jack has two luxury guest cottages that he recently finished. He is trying the working farm, Airbnb concept."

"They are quite nice, too," Pearl said. He said he was inspired by your villa, El Cielo in St. Ann."

"Except he was going for rustic chic," Philip said, "they are located on the other side of the farm, near the waterfalls. You know that's a good romantic spot."

"It's on top of a hill with an excellent view of the surrounding countryside and the sea in the distance. There's a hot tub on the patio," Pearl said dreamily. "You can make love under the stars."

"Which we did," Philip grinned and pulled Pearl to him.

"Get a room," Chex muttered. "I am adding newlyweds to my list of pet peeves."

Pearl laughed.

Philip looked at him, "Think about it, though, Chex. You'd be near your son for the summer, and Mom would be so over the moon happy to meet her grandson."

Chex frowned. "I don't want her in my child's life. She was useless in mine."

Philip sighed. "She is our mother; she is still here; at our age, it's a privilege to have a parent alive. Staying at Crimson Hills will allow you to reconcile with her and Garnet and get to know your son."

Chapter Nine

Chex went to his suite of rooms with that thought in his head. He couldn't believe he was toying with the idea of going back to Crimson Hills to stay for an extended period. Who would have thought the day would come when he voluntarily considered staying at Crimson Hills?

But he was just thinking about it; he didn't know if he would do it. He glanced at the clock; it was near seven-thirty.

The morning was overcast but still bright, yet his mind wouldn't settle down for him to sleep. He lay on his back, looked up at the ceiling, and tried not to castigate himself for being so stupid. He had done enough of that over the last five years. What he needed to do now was to plan strategy. He hadn't wanted children, but that was beside the point; he had a child whether he liked it or not, and there was no way he could successfully ignore that fact.

He had barely restrained himself through the years from

thinking about Garnet. Sometimes, at odd times, her face had flashed in his mind; he smelled a particular brand of perfume, and there she was. He had gotten cold and callous with women after she left. Before her, at least, he had been humane with his sexual encounters; after her, he had been brutal. To the point where he just didn't enjoy sex anymore. It felt mechanical and soulless. For the past two years, he had been willingly celibate.

It was two years ago when he had sought therapy after finding out that his close friend Madge was a murderess. It had shaken him to the core. Ironically, Duke, her husband, was the one who had insisted that they try therapy. Phillip was the one who had referred them to his therapist, Dr. Henry.

At first, it was all about Madge, his expectations of people, and how shocked he was about the events that unfolded. Then Dr. Henry started probing and prodding into his life, trying to find out what made him tick. He hadn't wanted to talk about his past.

"Well then, I can't help you further, Chex. I am uncomfortable taking your money, knowing you won't be helped. There are far less expensive ways to get this off your chest. You can simply talk to a friend. But you have some deep-seated issues. I can help you deal with them. I'll help you learn the skills to cope."

Chex knew he needed the help, so he decided to talk. "My father was obsessed with the end of the world. He bought a couple of acreages in the hills, and he and a couple of like-minded folks decided to wait things out in the bushes."

Dr. Henry nodded. Silently encouraging him.

"My mother was on a Jamaican tour; she was adventurous then. She was on a mission to find all the nooks and crannies in Jamaica that weren't so famous or well-visited but had their own brand of beauty.

"That's when she found Crimson Hills. She was twenty-one, fresh out of university with her History and Archaeology degree. She visited Knightsbridge; there is a waterfall there. She didn't know it was private property or that the owner, Maurice Knight, was an obsessed religious fanatic.

"And what do you know? She was bathing at the waterfall at the same time when he went there. They said it was love at first sight. I think it was good old-fashioned lust. Anyway, four weeks later, they were married. Nine months later, my mother had my oldest brother. She bought into his philosophy, religion, or whatever it was and stayed with him. As the years passed, my father got more unhinged; everything was a conspiracy, every event was an end-of-time event, and urgency to get prepared to be beamed up."

"Beamed up?" Dr. Henry asked.

"Yes," Chex nodded, "my father's theory was that he was some sort of Enoch figure. That he would be transported by aliens in spaceships who would take us to safety while the world burns. Any day would be the day. He had people on night watch. He punished those who did not live up to an imaginary list of virtues that could change daily. For the most part, I did not meet up with any of them."

"I see," Dr. Henry nodded. "What form did punishment take? Was he violent?"

"Not really. He was creative with his punishments. He was well-versed in torture, especially of little boys; he knew how to make us feel deprived, whether it was by food, sleep, restriction of movement, or sunlight."

"Sunlight?" Dr. Henry looked at him in disbelief.

"Yes," Chex inhaled roughly, "There was a house he called 'punishment house.' He boarded up the windows and had heavy padlocks on the doors. He carried the only key.

I was usually a candidate for 'punishment house' because I could not mask my utter contempt for the man. I would look into his crazy eyes, he would tell me something, and I would laugh, which further enraged him and would prolong whatever punishment he had planned for me.

"He used to tell me I wasn't going to be saved, and I told him I didn't want to go wherever he was going. I actively did the opposite of whatever he said because I genuinely didn't want to be in the same place as he would be for all eternity. If that was heaven, or a spaceship, or wherever, I wanted a hard pass."

Dr. Henry nodded. "I am getting a fuller picture of you now, Chex. Since childhood, you have been navigating a challenging and toxic environment, facing your father's eccentric beliefs and actions. It's clear that you developed a strong sense of resistance and a desire to distance yourself from his influence. How did you cope with such a difficult upbringing?"

"I had a broken piano. I fixed it," Chex sighed. "I had to use my creative muscles when in the dark. I daydreamed about a life beyond the one my father envisioned. I became adept at creating my own mental refuge; I did a lot of living in my head."

"What do you think was wrong with my father?" Chex asked. "From what you know about him as related by Phillip and myself, what's your best guess?"

Dr. Henry chewed over the question for a moment. "Well, it's impossible to say without treating him myself, but based on the information you've shared, it seems like your father may have suffered from a severe delusional disorder, possibly coupled with elements of narcissism. His fixation on apocalyptic scenarios, the belief in his own divine role, and the imposition of ever-changing virtues on those around him indicate a significant departure from reality."

"Could I have that same fixation on things or people? Could I inherit whatever it is he had?"

"It's natural to wonder about potential inherited traits. However, it's essential to understand that mental health conditions are complex and multifaceted. While certain disorders may have a genetic component, environmental factors also play a crucial role. Your resilience and ability to recognize and question your past experiences suggest a different path than your father's."

He continued, "Genetics can contribute to a predisposition, but it doesn't determine your destiny. Your personal experiences and choices all play significant roles in shaping who you are."

Chex nodded, "I became fixated on a girl once. I almost felt powerless under the emotions she evoked in me. She was all I could think about. I tried to play it cool, but I felt this underlying madness that threatened to overwhelm me. I have always sensed that I had a bit of what my father had. I just can't explain it."

"It's not uncommon for people to experience intense emotions, especially in matters of the heart," Dr. Henry said, "fixations and strong emotions don't necessarily equate to the severe delusions your father exhibited."

Chex sighed, "I don't want to end up like him. Even when I was fixated on that girl, I could sense this edge, this intensity that made me question if I had a grip on reality. It scared me."

Dr. Henry nodded understandingly. "It was your first time experiencing that emotion, I take it?"

"Yes," Chex nodded. I had never felt it before or since. She made me feel out of control, out of sorts. I really can't explain it."

The doctor nodded. "Chex, I think you are suffering from CPTSD. I diagnosed it in your brother and encouraged him to make you see me as well."

"Oh, you did, did you?" Chex muttered, "That's why he was so insistent that I needed to see a therapist. What on earth is CPTSD?"

"Complex Post-Traumatic Stress Disorder," Dr. Henry said, "it is a condition that can develop in response to prolonged exposure to trauma, particularly in interpersonal relationships. Unlike PTSD, which is often linked to a specific event, CPTSD is associated with chronic trauma, such as ongoing abuse or neglect, like what you went through in your childhood."

Chex's eyes widened as he absorbed the information. "So, what does it involve?"

"CPTSD encompasses a wide range of symptoms, including difficulties in emotional regulation, self-esteem issues, and challenges in forming and maintaining healthy relationships."

"Emotional regulation," Chex murmured, "I definitely had problems with that around her. What can be done about it? Can it be treated?"

"Absolutely," Dr. Henry replied. "Therapy, especially trauma-focused therapy, can be highly beneficial. It involves addressing the impact of past traumas, developing coping mechanisms, and fostering a more resilient mindset. Medication may also be considered in some cases, but the primary focus is therapeutic interventions."

Chex nodded thoughtfully. "I guess it makes sense. I've always felt haunted by my past, and sometimes, it feels like I'm on the verge of losing control. To this day, I cannot sleep in the dark or at night, and I sabotaged the one relationship that I had. I couldn't handle how she made me feel emotionally."

"Recognizing it is the first step," Dr. Henry said reassuringly. "By seeking help and understanding the factors at play, you're already taking control of your narrative. Remember, you have the power to shape your future, and with the right support, you can break the cycle. Your brother did. "

"But he was seeing you for five years!" Chex said.

"That's how long it took for him." Dr. Henry said.

Chex sighed, "Well, I guess it's time to face it head-on and not let it define me. I may even have a healthy relationship one day."

Dr. Henry nodded, "You will. I am sure that together, we can work towards healing and building a path forward that is uniquely yours."

****

When Chex opened his eyes again, he realized that one of Dr. Henry's therapeutic exercises had been narrative therapy. The doctor encouraged him to delve into the stories of his life, exploring not just the traumatic events but also the good times.

"Think of your life as a story, Chex," Dr. Henry would say. "And remember, you are the author. We can't change the past, but we can reshape how we interpret and integrate those experiences into our present and future."

The doctor would guide him through the process, helping him identify recurring themes, patterns, and the impact these narratives had on his sense of self.

Exploring his life story, he began to help him recognize the narratives he had carried from his past—stories of unworthiness, fear, and the haunting echoes of trauma.

Dr. Henry encouraged him to challenge and rewrite those narratives, emphasizing moments of strength, growth, and courage to confront his own vulnerabilities.

Chex discovered that narrative therapy wasn't about erasing the past but reframing it, allowing him to reclaim agency over his life story. Dr. Henry often reminded him, "You are not defined by the events that happened to you; you are defined by how you choose to interpret and respond to them."

He could do some therapy right now on himself. He couldn't continue self-medicating with drugs and alcohol the minute he felt himself spinning out of control.

He was past that now; he had the tools to cope. He had been seeing the doctor for eighteen months, and he could get through this rough patch.

He should have been able to handle all of this easily, his father's death, seeing Garnet again, and finding out he had a son without resorting to stimulants and going back to his old ways.

He should be able to think of the past without a good serving of self-revulsion. He just needed to relax.

Dr. Henry's voice came into his thoughts. "What you don't want to address, you suppress. And that leads to a downward spiral."

He closed his eyes, and for the first time in five years, he revisited his story with Garnet.

Chapter Ten

Sometime in the past

Chex pinched himself when he saw the girl walking into the studio to audition. Duke looked across at him and grinned.

"She is pretty," Duke murmured. Let's hope she can actually sing. You know, people tell pretty girls what they want to hear, even if it's not true. If she croaks, I am going to laugh."

Chex grinned. He watched as Lexi did her friendly chat and showed her to the sound booth. He was suddenly feeling nervous for her. He didn't want her to fail. He exhaled when she started singing. He had no need to be nervous. She blew them all away. Even Duke was nodding.

"She's good," Duke said. You could have given her the song to do by herself, and it would have made a splash."

"She's definitely in," Lexi said behind him. I expected it. She's a professional on the hotel circuit, and she's actually doing a music degree and has had voice training."

"What's her name?" Duke asked.

"Garnet Silver," Lexi said.

"That's her real name?" Chex asked.

"Yes," Lexi said.

"Sounds good. Maybe we should do a remix of 'No Promises' with her, Duke," Chex said. "And put it on the album."

"That would work," Duke nodded.

"She's getting nervous with us just staring at her," Chex said, "tell her we'll get in touch with her tomorrow and that she did good," he said to Lexi.

Their eyes met and something in Chex shifted. This was not normal. He forgot to breathe until she pulled her gaze away. Lexi gave her the speech about getting in touch, and she left. He found he couldn't wait to see her again.

"Let me see her file," he said to Lexi when she was gone.

Duke chuckled. "She's not your type."

"I know," Chex said. He looked over the standard questionnaire with her name, contact information, married or single—she had circled single. He smiled. He sat out the rest of the auditions, thinking about Garnet Silver.

"That's the last one," Lexi said after another outstanding singer left. "It seems as if we got most of the best singers on the last day in the last hour."

"I agree," Chex said. What's on the menu this evening? It's dinner time, and I could eat."

"Let me call downstairs," Lexi said, "do you want it sent up or…"

"I'll go down," Chex got up and stretched. "You guys deserve a break too."

"It's oxtail, curried goat, fried chicken," Lexi said, coming off the phone. "With all the sumptuous sides, we are definitely coming down."

When Chex got there, the dining room was fairly packed. There was a line at the buffet, but he wasn't in a rush, so he joined Sam, who was sitting at their usual table. Everyone knew it was reserved for them. Samuel Clark was his studio manager and head of his management team. They usually had informal dinner meetings, where Sam told him what was happening in the company outside of their official meetings in the office. Sam was just hanging up the phone when he sat down.

"That was Omar from security," he said to Chex. Apparently, there is a pretty lady in the parking lot. It looks like she's having car problems. Something about the key not turning in the ignition. She is waiting for her mechanic."

"Describe her," Chex said, "I know you asked for her stats."

"You know me well," Sam chuckled. "Short wavy hair, white top, blue jeans, slim but curvy in all the right places."

"That's Garnet Silver. She auditioned today," Chex got up.

"Where are you going?" Sam asked.

"The key not turning in the ignition is a simple fix. I'll help her."

"Okay," Sam nodded. "Bring her to dinner. I want to see her. Omar was practically beside himself with excitement when talking about her."

Chex frowned. "I don't think I want her exposed to you. She strikes me as a good girl."

"I love good girls," Sam protested. "And they love me!"

"That's the problem," Chex muttered.

He walked out of the building, wondering why he suddenly cared who Sam dated.

****

He put on the performance of his life over the next couple of months with Garnet. He tried treating her like a casual friend. But he didn't want her as a friend. He wanted her. He drove himself crazy with denial. He hoped that his mental conflict was not obvious to her. He found himself researching garnet stones and their significance. He commissioned one of his cousins, Lara Hastings, to custom design a necklace for a gift, a garnet in a silver setting.

"Lucky girl," Lara had murmured. "I have never known you to buy jewelry for a woman before now."

"I have never thought one deserved it before now," Chex said.

"Garnets make great engagement rings," Lara said. "They are not as durable as diamonds, but they can hold their own. They are just as gorgeous as their close cousin, rubies, and they kind of look the same. The symbolism is perfect: garnets symbolize love, passion, loyalty, and commitment."

"Who said anything about engagements?" Chex asked.

He had just had a conversation with Garnet about not minding if she slept with everyone in the building after almost driving himself crazy when she went on a date with Sam.

He had acted like it didn't matter, that she was just any girl, but here he was, getting a custom-made necklace done just because he couldn't stop thinking about her wearing it—a gift he would probably not give her.

"I thought that's why you asked for a garnet stone for the necklace," Lara said, "I always thought you were the type of person who played the field, and when you fall, you will fall hard. I have seen it so many times. The big bad tigers usually turn into domestic cats when they are in love."

"Her name is Garnet Silver," Chex said. "I thought I would give her a gift based on her name."

"Ah," Lara murmured, "she sounds lovely. If she has both garnet and silver precious stone traits, then she has an understated air of sophistication; she is classy without being too brash. She is good-looking, talented, and outgoing with a complex blend of passion, strength, and a hint of mystery."

"You just described her to a 't'," Chex said. "She is special."

"I know you, Chex. You don't buy a woman a symbolic necklace unless there's something more than a casual encounter."

"It's complicated," Chex said, "if I knew you were going to psychoanalyze me, I wouldn't ask you to make the necklace."

"Who else would you ask?" Lara laughed. "I am the best jewelry designer in Jamaica. Your problem is that you are trying to avoid your own feelings. Maybe this necklace is a way to express something you're not ready to put into words. Sometimes, actions speak louder than words."

"Okay," Chex sighed, "maybe you're right. It's just that everything feels so different with her. She's not like anyone I've met. By the way, we are not dating, nor have we even kissed."

"But she has gotten under your skin," Lara laughed. "Oh, my dear Chexy, take your time and let things unfold naturally. If Garnet is as remarkable as her name suggests, she might just be the exception to your rule. And in the meantime, I will design that engagement ring in anticipation of you reaching the ultimate conclusion that you love her and can't do without her."

"Wait a minute," Chex sputtered, "I am not paying for that."

"I don't expect you to pay for it now," Lara laughed. "But you will one day remember I have it here when you are ready."

****

He had taken his time, allowing things to unfold naturally. And then, he had to speed things up a little. He had missed her sorely since Duke's album launch and had a little panic attack when he thought he wouldn't see her again. So, he went to Montego Bay to check up on her and casually invited her to his Christmas party.

He held out for six weeks, allowing her to return to school. He stalked her by sending a detective to check up on her and give him daily reports. He called her every day to casually talk.

At the party, he gave her the necklace and pretended like it was a casual gift. As usual, she looked awesome stepping into the party venue, dressed for comfort over fashion in her red turtleneck dress. No skin on show, but he got an instant hard-on, which was remarkable because he hadn't been aroused lately.

He didn't even want to assess why Garnet, who was covered up to her neck, could arouse him. Yet, he was unmoved by the dozens of women around him shivering in the cold in their scanty attire. Garnet had well and truly captured his attention, and she didn't know how he felt.

He casually mentioned that he was celebrating her birthday all month in February, then asked her to stay with him for the whole month. He held his breath, waiting for her to tell him no. And when she did, he had a rebuttal: "I don't have to touch you, if you don't want me to." Luckily, she wanted him to.

Their first night together was still indelibly printed on his mind; she had branded him forever, and no woman before or since had made such an impact. His fears had been realized; he was in too deep. And for close to a year, he didn't care who knew. He was sitting in the audience at one of Duke's sold-out concerts, and when Garnet went up with him to sing "No Promises," he listened keenly to the words he had written two years ago: "In the city lights where shadows dance, whispers in the wind taking a chance. Walking down the street, lost in reverie. No Promises tonight, just you and me."

It struck him that he wanted to make promises to her and keep them, but he was terrified, and that sense of terror and absolute helplessness sent him to sabotage their relationship.

He broke up with her when she was in the middle of planning her back-to-school itinerary. He only saw her again a few months later when she came to the office to pick up her royalty cheque on the Friday before her birthday.

Sam was flirting with her.

And he had seen red. He had spent a few months vacillating between wanting to call her and grovel, wondering if she was seeing anyone and if she had moved on. The realization that he had made a mistake gnawed at him daily, but pride and fear kept him from reaching out. Yet, seeing her with someone else brought an unexpected surge of jealousy and regret.

He met her in the parking lot before she went into her car.

Sensing his presence, Garnet looked up and met his gaze. The air seemed to crackle with tension between them.

"Chex," she ran her fingers through her hair, "what's up?"

"I want to have a lost weekend. I want to forget that we broke up. I want to make love to you all weekend. I don't want to talk. I just want to feel."

Garnet swallowed. "I don't think that's a good idea."

He ran his unsteady hands across his face. "Maybe not. I miss you."

"I miss you too," Garnet whispered. "Honestly, I could have had the cheque sent to my account."

"I know." Chex took a deep breath. His vulnerability lay bare. "I was a fool, Garnet. Breaking up with you was the biggest mistake of my life. I was scared, and I let my fears control me. If you spend the weekend with me, I'll do it again. I am making no promises here; this is a one-off."

Garnet studied him for a moment, her eyes searching his face. "I've spent months trying to move on, but I miss you, I miss us. I'll come over. I didn't plan for a weekend away. I don't have any clothes or…"

"Doesn't matter; we won't need any," Chex said hoarsely.

"I am not on birth control," Garnet warned.

"I'll take care of that," Chex said.

That had been one of the most intense weekends of his life. They were sexually compatible, but what made it so intense was the fact that she laid his emotions bare in a way that no one else ever had. He was too out of control.

In the quiet hours of that first night, Chex found himself listening to the rhythmic cadence of Garnet's breathing. Deep down, he knew he was going to have to let her go, and he cried.

Chapter Eleven

"**M**r. Hastings," Marjorie popped her head around the office door, "Dr. Henry is here to see you." Chex threw his stress ball up in the air and caught it. "I don't want to see him. I am busy."

"You don't look busy," Dr. Henry said above her shoulder, "I'm here already."

"I didn't know you made office calls," Chex smirked, "or I would have taken advantage of that when you were my therapist. Do you hear the 'were' in that sentence, Dr. Henry?"

Dr. Henry came into the office and closed the door.

"I'm quite aware that you are put out with me, Chex, but it has been a week since the funeral. You were doing well and making strides, and going to your father's funeral was not a bad call. I assessed that you were at a stage of your therapy where you could handle it."

"I didn't go to the funeral," Chex said, still throwing his ball in the air. "I couldn't do it; on approaching Knightsbridge, I think I had a panic attack."

Dr. Henry sat across from him. "That is not unexpected. It is your first time back there in years."

Chex sighed and squeezed the stress ball. "As soon as I got close, the memories flooded back, and I felt this overwhelming dread."

"Knightsbridge holds a lot of painful memories for you, Chex. It's okay to feel overwhelmed. Facing such a significant source of trauma is a challenging step, and it's common for strong emotions to surface."

"I didn't expect it to hit me so hard. I feel like I'm regressing, like all my progress is slipping away." Chex said, "I even did some narrative therapy last night, and I still feel out of sorts, troubled."

"Progress in therapy isn't always linear," Dr. Henry said. There are ups and downs. Setbacks are a natural part of the process. What matters is that you recognize them and continue to work through them."

"The funeral was just the tip of the iceberg," Chex said. "When I was having a panic attack, I asked my driver to take me to a restaurant. While I was sitting there and contemplating what to do next, in walked Garnet Silver. Remember her?"

"How could I forget? She is a major part of your story."

"Well, she has a child, a boy. He is five, he is mine, and he looks just like my dad."

"Interesting," Dr. Henry said.

"That's all you are going to say?" Chex growled. "Aren't you going to ask how it made me feel seeing her again or how I feel knowing that I have a child when I didn't want children?"

Dr. Henry leaned back in his chair, his gaze steady on

Chex. "Discovering you have a child is undoubtedly a significant revelation that can stir up many emotions. It's natural to feel overwhelmed, confused, and even conflicted in such a situation."

"I was conflicted earlier, not anymore. I spent a whole week self-medicating." Chex sighed, "As I said, I regressed."

Dr. Henry winced.

"And then it occurred to me, after all the turbulent emotions running around in my mind, that there are a few sure things in all of it. I want her back. I haven't had a truly happy day since we broke up, and even though I didn't think I wanted children, he is here, and I want to be in my son's life. I want to be the type of father to him that I never had. I want them both."

"How were you planning to accomplish this?" Dr. Henry asked. "Are they living in Crimson Hills?"

Chex nodded.

"So what's the plan?"

"Go there temporarily," Chex cleared his throat. "My brother has guest cottages at Knightsbridge."

"Go for it," Dr. Henry said. "I have been trying to get you to go to that place and to use the tools we have practiced in therapy. You need to realize that Knightsbridge is just a place; how you react to it can be altered. I would suggest that you even visit Punishment House. Go in there and stand in the middle of the room. Have conversations with your mother. Clear the air, Chex, and take charge of your story. You are ready."

Chex inhaled. "Just a week ago, I had a panic attack."

"Panic attacks are a natural response to overwhelming stress and anxiety," Dr. Henry continued. "But they don't define you. They signal that something within you needs attention, and facing those triggers, like Punishment House, can be a way to understand and process those emotions."

Chex nodded. "It's hard to confront the memories and the pain."

"I know, but you've made incredible progress in our sessions. Remember, Knightsbridge is just a location; it has no real power over you. By facing it, you reclaim control over your reactions and emotions. You will have a healthier relationship with Garnet because of it."

Chex nodded. "I guess it's time to stop running away."

"I am happy you came to that conclusion, Chex, because that will fit into my plans perfectly."

"So you weren't here for a session?" Chex asked wryly.

"No," Dr. Henry said. "A colleague of mine, Dr. Charles Payne, envisioned creating a mental health documentary. His idea was to feature patients with chronic mental illnesses like schizophrenia, bipolar disorder, obsessive-compulsive disorder, and complex post-traumatic stress disorder, highlighting their journeys, challenges, and triumphs. He believed that sharing these personal stories could increase awareness, reduce stigma, and foster a better understanding of mental health issues in the broader community."

"I am not telling people about my trauma and subsequent disorder," Chex said.

"Why not?" Dr. Henry raised an eyebrow.

"Because we don't talk about these things in Jamaica, especially men and especially people in my profession. In the music fraternity, we have an image to maintain. Being mentally unstable for whatever reason is not a good look. You keep that kind of thing on the down low."

Dr. Henry nodded. "I know. That is why when Dr. Payne came to me with his idea, I was eager to jump on board. Mental health issues are still a stigma in this country and not widely accepted in the black community as a whole.

"And definitely frowned upon in certain jobs. I have so many patients in the clergy and the political arena who are absolutely terrified of making their mental health issues known."

"At least they came to you for help," Chex said. "They should be applauded for that. Sorry, we should be applauded for that."

"I suppose," Dr. Henry said. "I didn't want you to participate in the documentary, Chex. We are oversubscribed; we have tons of raw footage and want it arranged and edited. I am unclear about the actual term for it, but we want it polished and finished, divided into three one-hour slots, and ready to be viewed."

"The word you are looking for is post-production," Chex said. "We do that here."

"Could you personally handle it?" Dr. Henry asked. "I think looking at other people's journeys and hearing their setbacks and successes could be useful. And I also heard that you are one of the best people to give it the treatment it deserves. While asking around, your company name kept coming up."

Chex grinned. "I'll do it. I'll even give you a discount."

"Did I mention that Dr. Payne happens to live in Crimson Hills, has his practice in Montego Bay, and is the liaison on this?"

"No, you did not," Chex said wearily.

"How hard would it be for you to do this in Crimson Hills while trying to reconnect with Garnet? Would you need loads of equipment or personnel?"

"Well, it's post-production. I'd need a good computer setup, editing software, and a reliable internet connection. Fortunately, the nature of post-production work allows for flexibility in terms of location. I can work remotely."

"Good," Dr. Henry nodded and got up. "I will email you Dr. Payne's contacts; he will discuss payment with you and all the nuts and bolts for the endeavor. I will speak to you on Thursday at our usual session time. I guess we will have to do it online."

"Wait a minute," Chex said. "I fired you, remember."

"You still need me," Dr. Henry said. "The job together is not yet complete."

Chapter Twelve

Her father was due home on Tuesday evening. They had divvied up the tasks for his homecoming party by the poolside. She was responsible for the music, per her aunt's instructions; it was supposed to be seventies Jamaican music, as her father loved music from that era.

She had fun putting together the playlist, which included songs by Jimmy Cliff, Burning Spear, The Wailers, and Third World. She played and replayed the tunes, and Patti sang along with her.

Patti was responsible for the minimal decorations: blue and silver balloons and a festive centerpiece for the long trestle table, while Garwin and Erin were responsible for the food, a wide array of finger foods that they kept trotting out from their townhouse in warmers.

She had tasked Neon with writing welcome home on a banner. He had done that and decided to spruce it up with little dinosaurs all over the paper. He was in his creative zone.

"Our first Silver family get-together," Garnet said.

"Before you know it, we will quickly turn into the Nelsons," Patti grinned.

"I wouldn't mind if we had that kind of family culture; I've always envied how close-knit they are," Erin said. "We could one-up them with the entertainment, too. We have some chefs and musicians; our get-togethers should be on another level. We should invite the Smoke and Silver band to provide live entertainment for our next family event."

"And Garnet can sing," Patti said, "and Gersham can play the sax."

"Oh yes," Garnet nodded. "But Garwin can sing too. Have you ever heard your husband?"

"Oh yes," Erin nodded, "he likes to sing to me in bed."

"Stop telling people our intimate secrets," Garwin came out with a cupcake tower.

Erin laughed.

"By the way," Garwin said, "this is courtesy of Jill. She heard Sterling was coming out of rehab today and wanted to contribute to the party."

"That was so sweet of her," Patti said. "Isn't she eight months pregnant? I thought Larry told her to take it easy."

"It's Jill; she'll probably work until delivery day," Garwin shrugged. "Besides, she heard Dad was coming out of rehab and wanted to do something to contribute to the dinner. Remember how she hired Dad, fussed over him, and made sure he wasn't drinking? If he was, she would report it to us. Jill was constantly checking up on Dad. We should have invited her."

"But it was the general consensus that this homecoming was only for close family," Garnet pointed out, "and if we were going to start inviting people based on how kind they've been to Dad, the whole town would be here."

"True," Patti said, "you'd have to invite Maud and Willie."

"And the whole Nelson family, not just Jill," Erin said. "All of them, especially Aunt Bunny, has been good to you guys."

"Okay," Garwin held up his hand. "Maybe we should do a Crimson Hill party at the restaurant and make it a giant thank you to everyone for being good to us."

"That would be a good idea," Patti said. "I've been thinking about doing something on a broad scale. I started my lifestyle blog, writing ordinary people's stories. Then, while talking to people, I find that some people could use a helping hand."

"My friend Carmelita runs a charity called Caring Connections. They sponsor orphans up to the tertiary level with schooling. The Nelsons build houses for people who need them. We, the Silvers, have been blessed beyond our wildest dreams. We should do something, too."

"I agree," Garnet said. "Our family was once the poorest in these parts."

"Yes," Garwin nodded. "Garnet may not remember this, but there were times we had no clothes, no shoes, no food, no…"

"That's it!" Patti got up. "That's what I was thinking of doing. We could set up a food bank, have a central area to drop off clothing items, and then identify those in the community who need it and distribute these items on a personal level. We can do a Christmas treat, a Summer Jam, or a back-to-school party."

"That will clash with Aunt Bunny's," Garwin said. "She always has a back-to-school party."

"No clashing," Patti shook her head. "I will recruit all the do-gooders under our charity umbrella, and we will enlarge and enhance their activities."

"You could name it Silver Lining," Garnet said. "Every dark cloud has one."

"Oh my," Erin looked at her approvingly. "That sounds good."

"I love it," Patti nodded.

"And then Gersham called her. 'We are three minutes away; I hope everything is set.'"

"Yes," Garnet said, "Neon has transformed the welcome home banner. I hope Dad doesn't mind being greeted by drunk dinosaurs in lurid colors."

****

Garnet couldn't believe how different her father looked. He appeared taller, more muscular, and more youthful than she had ever seen him. But what was even more striking was his attitude. It was as if he had undergone a personality transplant. He was jovial and witty, with no traces of the downtrodden, silent ghost of a man that she used to know.

Her aunt was the one who showed him around while they stood around waiting for his opinion.

"What do you think, Dad?" Gersham asked after Sterling went around inspecting the interior of his townhouse. "Would you like to stay here or back at the original place?"

Sterling stood with his hands akimbo. "Here, of course. It is beyond my wildest dreams. I tell you the truth, this is the desired outcome if someone is going to steal from you and you get back your thing. Getting it back looking a hundred times better than before is just poetic justice."

They all chuckled politely.

Garwin and Gersham took his suitcases and some painting paraphernalia out of the car.

"Where should I put these?" Garwin asked.

"In the room overlooking the pool," Sterling stood at the patio doors.

"Joy chuckled. He has developed a talent for painting, and he has some good pieces, too."

"Thank you, sis," Sterling smiled. "In rehab, they encourage creativity. I found that painting was my activity of choice. I have a natural knack for it."

"Let's go by the poolside," Garwin said. "I don't want the food to dry out in the warmer."

"Yes, please," Neon tugged on her dress.

"We should wait for everyone," Garnet said.

"No, let's eat," Sterling said. "I missed your cooking, Garwin."

Garwin smiled.

"And yours too, Gersham," Sterling hurriedly added.

"Wait until you taste Erin's cooking," Gersham said. "People keep saying she has an edge over us."

Sterling grinned, "I am so sorry I missed your wedding."

"It was understandable," Erin said. "We all want you to get well."

They walked to the poolside.

"Okay," Joy said. "Let us say a prayer, and then let us eat."

"I'll pray," Sterling said, "but before that, I have a speech."

He cleared his throat. "Let me just say I'm very grateful to have you children. We all know I have not been the best father. But once there is life, there can be change. And I'm feeling optimistic that I can still make some kind of impact in your lives. I am grateful for all of you, and I hope that moving forward, we can have better relationships than we had before. Alcohol addiction is a lifelong struggle.

"As I embark on this journey of recovery, I ask for your patience, understanding, and support. I promise to do my best to be there for you, to be present and sober, and to make amends for my past mistakes. Thank you for giving me this chance to change, grow, and be a better father, grandfather, and brother. Let us pray for strength, guidance, and a brighter future together."

They held hands in a circle, and Sterling prayed.

Joy was wiping away tears when he was done.

Garnet determinedly kept her eyes averted from her aunts. She knew if she looked at her, she would tear up, too.

But it seemed as if everybody was trying not to look at each other.

"Let's eat," Garwin said huskily.

****

The party was in full swing, with the smooth, sweet melodies of Beres Hammond's seventies album playing in the background. They were sitting at the table, Sterling was talking and laughing. It was unlike the father she had grown up seeing. Garnet had to pinch herself occasionally, and then the conversation turned to Leonard Crooks.

"He was found guilty of all three murders," Joy said. "The sentencing hearing is in six weeks. They should just sentence him at the same time. Why the long wait?"

"I want to be at that sentencing hearing," Sterling said.

"Me too," Joy nodded. "They should lock him up and throw away the key. Our mother will finally get some justice, even if it is thirty years late."

"I was theorizing," Patti said. "If they gave him thirty years for each girl, that would be ninety years. He's, what, sixty? He would never see the light of day."

"Nah," Erin said. "I want them to say blatantly, life in prison, with no possibility of parole. I don't know how they calculate prison years, but thirty is not really thirty literal years, and they do from time to time let out people because of good behavior and whatnot."

Garnet nodded. "I agree. I want him to have no hopes of coming out. However, I would like some leniency shown to Madge."

"Madge is the girl who carried out the killings," Sterling frowned. "You know her?"

"Yes," Garnet nodded. I do. I thought I had known her well, but you never really know what people are capable of when cornered, do you?"

Sterling nodded. "True."

Chapter Thirteen

Garnet sat down tiredly. Her aunt was teaching seventies dance moves. Some of the moves were too energetic for her.

Sterling came to join her.

"I've been curious," Sterling said. "Who is little Maurice's father?"

"His name is Neon, Dad, not Little Maurice," Garnet said.

"He got nothing from the Silver side of the gene pool." Sterling chuckled. "Not a thing. Maybe your next one will be more Silver than Knight."

"I'm not planning on having any more. Garwin and Gersham will give you little Silvers."

Sterling chuckled. "I figure Laurel won't let Neon out of her sight, especially now that Maurice is gone."

"I haven't introduced him to that side of his family," Garnet said, "I just recently told everyone who his father is. And it was two weeks ago that his father found out about him."

"Oh," Sterling nodded.

"Tell me about Maurice Knight," Garnet said. "You said you knew him from when he was a child?"

"Oh, yes," Sterling said. "We went to the same prep school down the hill. The Knight family has always had that section of land on the other side, but they didn't live in Crimson Hills. They lived in the town, but he came here for school. Maurice was a quiet guy, not very talkative. The girls loved him. And then he got caught up with this religious group. I don't remember their names now. I don't remember many things, but I remember feeling very concerned about Maurice. I was the one who inadvertently caused him and Laurel to meet."

"How so?" Garnet asked.

"She was doing her Jamaican tour, going from parish to parish and seeking out the most beautiful spots. She ended up here, staying at Crimson Rest. I passed her one morning while heading to work. I gave her a lift down the road and told her about the waterfalls on the Knight property. Apparently, she went there, and they saw each other, and that was it. History was made. Love at first sight."

"Maurice was a terrible father to Chex," Garnet said, "the things he told me when we were dating…"

Sterling sighed. "Sometimes I wonder who is worse, me or Maurice. We both made a mess of our families. Anyway, onto more positive things. What are you doing back here?"

"Finishing up school," Garnet said.

"Ah," Sterling nodded. "That's good; your grandmother would be proud of you; she was heavily into education."

"I just have one project to do, a documentary of all things," Garnet said. "I'm still undecided as to which topic to choose." "Did they give you options?" Sterling asked.

"Nope," Garnet sighed. "They left it up to us to figure

it out. What they did was give us an imposing sounding guideline.

She whipped out her phone and read the project guideline for him. "The final project should demonstrate a combination of technical skills, artistic creativity, and a deep understanding of both disciplines.

"The project should showcase the student's ability to integrate music and film effectively, resulting in a cohesive and compelling audiovisual experience. It should be original and creative; the student must demonstrate technical proficiency in music and film production. This includes skills such as audio recording, mixing, and mastering music, as well as cinematography, editing, and sound design for film."

"The student must," Garnet snickered, "'they have the 'must' in bold and underlined," she continued, "integrate music and film elements to create a unified and immersive experience, synchronizing music with on-screen action, and using sound to enhance storytelling. The project should demonstrate a high level of aesthetic and production value."

"In addition to the creative work itself, the student will make a presentation reflecting on their artistic choices, the effectiveness of their integration of music and film, and what they have learned throughout the process."

"Okay then," Sterling murmured. "How many years did they give you to do this?"

Garnet laughed. "Eight weeks. The deadline is mid-August. I don't want to do anything too complicated that will have me tearing out my hair. One location would be nice, and a manipulation of some copyright-free music would be even better."

"How long should it be?" Sterling asked.

"Thirty minutes," Garnet said. "That, in itself, is going to be a challenge. They are seriously testing my editing skills."

Sterling nodded.

"I told her to do the time travel angle," Gersham pulled up a chair. "Interview Maud Beecher, let her tell her stories."

"What's so interesting about that?" Patti asked, joining them with a slice of cake and sitting beside Gersham. "I think your family's story is infinitely more interesting. You didn't even know your mother's real name or family background until a few years ago. Your father went to jail for killing her even though her body was never found."

"I don't know if I want that immortalized on video," Gersham frowned. "Samir Chan literally blacklisted you in the media because of your article. I think our family story should stay here. I don't want Garnet to be a target."

Garnet smiled, unable to imagine a day when Gersham was not extra protective of her.

"But we have more than one intriguing family tale," Garwin and Erin joined the discussion.

"Yes, we do," Joy said, drifting closer. "Our mother's death will forever remain unsolved and untried. The monster who killed her was only caught because he killed others."

"I don't know if I want her story told," Sterling fretted. "It doesn't really portray her in a good light. She was the older woman who should have known better than to marry a boy younger than her children. We were the laughingstock of this community at one time."

"But nobody was laughing when my mother mysteriously died," Joy said, "and her story was more than her one-year marriage to Leonard Crooks. She single-handedly grew her chemical business after her husband died, raised us as a single mother, and made us the wealthiest family in Crimson Hills all on her own."

"It is a nice story," Garnet said, "but I don't think it can stand alone. Leonard Crook's conviction and soon-to-be sentencing adds interest, but everybody is discussing this."

"Then make it part of a broader story," Patti said, "do a Crimson Hill story, where you focus on the various people in this intriguing neighborhood."

"Yes," Garwin nodded, "take Derrick and Cindy; they were high school sweethearts who always knew they would be together. All of us in that friendship group figured that if anyone was going to end up with their childhood love, it would be them. But then Derrick married Nicky, that's Cindy's best friend. He did it for a green card. It was supposed to be a business marriage, but they had a child together, which meant that more than business was involved. So, Cindy and Derrick broke up."

"But aren't they together now?" Garnet asked, confused. "I saw them just two days ago."

"That's the intriguing part of it," Garwin said, "Derrick and Nicky divorced, and then Derrick comes back to Jamaica for Cindy, and in the process, finds out that his child with Nicky was not his but for his brother, Orandy, who he hadn't even met."

"Do you think they will tell me this for a documentary?" Garnet widened her eyes. "This is sort of sounding like a daytime soap."

"They might," Garwin said. "Nicky ended up marrying Orandy, Derrick's brother, and she and Cindy have been hanging out again. The brothers are close. Derrick said family get-togethers have ceased to be awkward."

"Oh my," Garnet murmured.

"I think you should do the documentary on people in this town who were wrongfully incarcerated," Erin said. "Your father, Dacy Bishop. Remember her? She and Lee Wiley have the best romantic story, hands down. He waited for her while in prison. And then it was found out that her brother, who she supposedly killed, faked his death and made it look like Dacy did it. To this day, my blood boils when I think about it."

"Yep, mine too," Patti said. "Her father treated her like she wasn't his, all while still having an affair with her mother."

"Good Lord," Garnet muttered. "I can't keep up. What's Dacy doing these days?"

"I think she is pregnant. She has a cute little bump," Patti said. "I saw her in Wimple's bakery the other day. She and Jill are pregnant; you know they are already planning playdates with their kids and stuff; those two have always been close. I am happy for Dacy. She is living a quiet life with her hubby, who loved her enough to wait for her while she was in prison. You have to feature them."

"They are not as compelling as Jack and Cambria," Garwin said. Jack escaped Knightsbridge and his father and went to Kingston to stay with his brothers, one of whom was Garnet's lover."

"It has been established, Garwin, that Neon's father is Jack's brother, Maurice's son. Everyone knows now, including him," Garnet sighed. "The secret is out. Give it a rest."

"I'd love to meet Neon's father," Sterling said. "At one time, Maurice had his whole family under lock and key. The boys were homeschooled. The older two escaped him as soon as they could. Why did Jack stay?"

"He didn't want to leave his mother alone with Maurice," Garwin said. "And Maurice dangled the ownership of the farm in his face, all while controlling his money. Jack had to go and ask for money for every little thing he wanted."

"The more I hear about Maurice, the more I am glad I didn't go to his funeral," Garnet said.

"He was awful to Jack. I urged him to leave," Garwin said. I told him that was no way to live. He heeded my advice and the advice of all his friends and left. In Kingston, he decided to go to a nightclub in the ghetto with his brother Chex. Do you know him, Garnet?"

"Yes," Garnet gritted out. "A little too well."

"And Chex decided that Jack needed to lose his virginity, so he arranged for it to happen. The brothel owner was Cambria's adopted sister, and she decided to force Cambria to work for her that night. It's a long story, but that's how they met."

"Oh wow," both Erin and Garnet said at the same time.

"They never had sex that night," Garwin said. "Both of them resented the situation, but they hung out and, over the months, got to know each other. Then Jack came home when Maurice had a stroke, and in the process, fell into a well and lost his memory. When Cambria didn't hear from him, she followed him here and, in the process, found out that she was Derrick and Lee Wiley's sister. Her mother, Chevelle, had given her up for adoption and didn't tell anyone."

"My goodness," Joy said. "If you put their story in a book, I would read it. A documentary wouldn't do it justice."

"And that's if they would even want to put their lives out there like that," Garnet said. "I am back to square one."

"No," Patti said. "Nobody has mentioned Mercedes' husband, Charles. He is Maud Beecher's lost son. There isn't a day that went by when you talked to Maud in the past where she wouldn't mention how her son was stolen. Everyone thought she was crazy for thinking so, including Mercedes. When Mercedes became Maud's therapist and asked her for a picture of her baby son, she found how similar he looked to Charles, her colleague whom she met at a work camp. And then found out that he was, in fact,

Maud's son."

"And we are back to time travel," Gersham grinned. "You can't do a story with Maud in it and not mention her time travel claims. You can't avoid it, Garnet, just give in."

Garnet laughed. "I am trying to simplify my life."

"Winter Wesson would be an easy, intriguing topic," Sterling said. "I'd watch it if you did it on him."

"The founder of Crimson Hill Great House?" Garnet frowned. "What's so interesting about him?"

"He has a load of adventures," Sterling chuckled. "He is a fascinating fellow. I spoke to him myself last year. I was helping Willie with something over the Great House, and he was there."

"Dad," Garnet groaned. "Winter Wesson died in the eighteenth century."

"But according to Maud," Erin said, "no literature has proven any such thing. He disappeared at the age of thirty-two... poof into thin air."

"I can believe it," Sterling nodded. "I spoke to the man, just like I am talking to you."

"You are pulling my leg," Garnet laughed.

"No," Sterling said seriously, "he was explaining to me that the sundial was a portal, some ancient tech that could time travel. He was still figuring out how to use it. He bought it from some person in Jerusalem. That man has traveled the world."

"Are you being serious?" Garnet asked her father.

"Yes," Sterling nodded. "I didn't mention it before because Maud told me not to; people do ridicule her for her time travel stories, and I wouldn't be a reliable witness because I was the town drunk, who would listen to me, but if you could get Winter Wesson on camera, that would be something."

"I don't believe it was him you saw," Garnet said. "Maybe

somebody was imitating him, and Maud and Willie were in on it."

"Maybe," Sterling said, "but that would make a good story."

"Can I tell you this has not helped me one bit?" Garnet looked at her family. "I am just as confused as to where to start."

"Do all of them," Patti said, "start with Winter Wesson, the town's founder, and squeeze in all the stories you can with everyone around town. I can guarantee you that it will be a great documentary."

Chapter Fourteen

Garnet spent all night trying to come up with an outline. She took Patti's advice and combined all the exciting stories in Crimson Hills. She even had a topic in her head: Crimson Hill Stories.

She would need a narrator. She could use Patti; her sister-in-law was a trained journalist. She would start at Crimson Hill Great House. If she could get the imitator Winter Wesson, he could talk about the place when he first arrived. Then, she would have a historian give a rundown of the families who were here originally and just have people sit down and tell their stories.

It would be a good documentary; she could feel it. She could barely wait for morning to go to Crimson Hill Great House.

She knocked on her aunt's door before she left. "I will be interviewing you and Dad as well," Garnet said, "Fern Silver's story deserves an airing, too."

"What time is it?" her aunt groaned. "And why are you up already?"

"You would be getting ready for the gym if you were in Kingston," Garnet laughed. "I barely slept last night. I've been working on my outline. First, I go to Crimson Hill Great House, and then later, I go door to door to the good citizens of this community and beg them to tell me their stories. Then I'll make appointments to see them and tape them."

Her aunt blinked at her owlishly.

"What I am getting at is, could you watch Neon for me and get him ready for school?"

"Sure," Joy murmured. "Have fun."

"What time can you do an interview before you go?" Garnet asked.

"Anytime," Joy murmured, sounding half asleep.

Garnet chuckled. That sleepy acceptance may be overturned when she was fully awake.

At least Maud was eager to help. She had been in her rose garden when Garnet drove up.

"That's a splendid idea for a documentary," Maud said.

"You haven't, by any chance, watched it before, have you?" Garnet asked, "During your time travels?"

Maud laughed. "If I did, I wouldn't tell you."

"My dad said there was a Winter Wesson imitator around here last year, and he said he would be back in June. I'd like to interview him when he gets here."

"That's a Good idea," Maud said. "He knows more about the great house and the area than anyone."

Garnet frowned. "I am skeptical about him being the real Winter Wesson. Will his information even be accurate?"

"I can always get you a history book and some of Winter Wesson's diaries to corroborate," Maud said. "I would be surprised if you weren't skeptical."

"Could you tell him I want to speak to him when he arrives? He is number one on my list."

"Sure," Maud nodded.

"I want to interview you too. I want the story of your missing baby and how you found him as an adult,"

"Sure, I am going to be on television," Maud cackled. "I love it."

"I love your response," Garnet said. "I am kind of nervous about asking many more people."

"They'll say yes," Maud assured her. "They'll tell you their stories."

"Is that something you know for sure?" Garnet asked.

"Yes," Maud nodded, "you are one of us, not a stranger. Of course, we'll tell you our story. Stay right there; I will get the books for you."

Garnet pondered who to approach first after leaving the great house.

Jill was the logical choice; she was the nicest person in Crimson Hills. She wouldn't tell her no.

She found Jill and Dacy at the bakery, having breakfast together. The place was not yet opened for business. She knocked on the door, and Jill opened it for her.

"You are so gorgeous," Jill said when she saw Garnet. "Like really pretty. You won the genetics lottery, for sure."

"She could model," Dacy added. "No, not model. The world does not deserve you."

Garnet laughed. "How are you two?"

"Pregnant!" they both said, giggling together.

"Do you want to eat with us?" Jill asked, sitting down again.

"I already had something," Garnet replied, sitting beside Jill. "You are big. Are you carrying twins?"

"No," Jill said. "I asked the doctor to make sure. But this baby is huge, and I can't wait to have him."

"It's a boy!" Garnet smiled. "Congrats. What are you having, Dacy?"

"A girl," Dacy said.

"All the best with your delivery."

"Thanks, hun," Dacy said, looking at her. "What is it? You look like you want to ask something."

"I do. I am doing a documentary about the stories in Crimson Hill, and I would like to know if you would contribute.

"Sure," Dacy nodded.

"And you too, Jill," Garnet turned to her.

"Me?" Jill widened her eyes.

"Yes, you. You lost a ton of weight and married the town's bad boy. Why did a nice girl like you marry Larry Nelson?"

"Dr. Larry Nelson," Dacy corrected and chuckled.

"Oh yes, I heard Larry just loves to be reminded that he has a Ph.D.," Garnet smiled. I can't wait to hear how that came about, too. Can you convince him to do the interview with you?"

"Sure," Jill nodded.

"And can I get Lee to join you, Dacy?"

"I suppose," Dacy said.

"Whew," Garnet exhaled. "Let me cross you two off the list. What time can I interview you?"

"We'll have to synchronize schedules with the husbands," Dacy said.

"Thank you, guys," Garnet said. "I have a couple more people on my list. I am hoping this will go as easy."

Unfortunately for her, it wasn't. Most people were heading off to work, so she decided to give it a rest until the evening. She had stopped looking and was on her way to the restaurant to pick up lunch when she saw Derrick Wiley parking in the parking lot at Crimson Rest. Cindy was with him, and she was carrying a giant cake box. She made a U-turn and drove into the parking lot behind them.

She had to shout through the car window to get their attention. "Cindy! Derrick!"

They both stopped and waited for her. "I wanted to talk to you both…" she said hurriedly.

"We are throwing a surprise birthday party for Chevelle," Cindy said. "She'll be here any minute now. Come join us, and when we are done, we can talk."

"Chevelle is your mom, isn't she?" she asked Derrick.

"Yes," Derrick nodded.

"Are all your siblings going to be there?" she asked.

"Not really, just those of us nearby," Derrick said. "Lee, Dacy, Cambria, and Jack. She's leaving this evening for a few days. So we thought we'd throw her a party while she is here."

"Oh, cool," Garnet nodded. She did not refuse to attend their intimate family party. A good chunk of her interview list would be there anyway.

The party was in full swing by the poolside. They even had an MC.

She didn't recognize the MC, but he widened his eyes when he saw her coming in with Cindy and Derrick.

Chevelle was well and truly surprised. At the MC's request, she stood up to make a speech.

"I would never have thought that I was attending a surprise birthday party at lunchtime. You got me, guys; you got me good. I feel so blessed. Every day, when I get up, I open my eyes, and I feel gratitude. I am grateful that I am here, I am grateful for my family, and I am especially thankful to my husband for making every day count. I love you madly, babe."

"Love you too," Othneil said, raising his glass.

Garnet was confused. They had grown children; why did they still look so in love?

She was sitting near Cindy, and she leaned over to speak to her. "Why are Derrick's parents so happy together after all these years? They look like newlyweds."

"That's because they are newlyweds. They found each other again after many years."

"Sounds like a good story," Garnet murmured.

"You have no idea," Cindy chuckled. "What was it you wanted to talk to me about?"

"Well, I…" Garnet was interrupted by Jack.

"Oh hey, Jack," Garnet smiled. "I haven't seen you for a while. Is that Cambria?"

"Yes," Jack nodded. "I should introduce you two. I didn't know you knew Chevelle."

"I don't," Garnet said. "I don't know half the people here. I was going to tell Cindy that I wanted to do a documentary on the people of Crimson Hills and their interesting stories. It's for school, my final project."

"Oh," Cindy said.

"My family told me some of the stories from here, and I must confess I am intrigued. Dacy and Jill already consented to be interviewed, and I wouldn't mind hearing about you and Derrick and Jack and Cambria," Garnet said.

Cindy smiled. "Well, I'll do it."

"I don't know," Jack said.

"Come on," Cindy urged him. "Help her out; it's to finish up college. I am proud of you for wanting to finish up," Cindy looked at her, her eyes sincere. I remember when you were just a little girl. My goodness, I must be getting old."

Garnet laughed, "You are just six years older than me,

Cindy."

"I know, but we took turns babysitting you when it was Garwin's turn to watch you after school. Do you remember us playing in your hair, styling it in elaborate styles?"

Garnet chuckled. "Vaguely."

"You were so inquisitive and precocious," Cindy chuckled. "You kept us on our toes, I tell you."

"I am still that inquisitive girl. I'll be asking close personal questions for the documentary," Garnet said.

"I have nothing to hide," Cindy said. "Derrick and I went through a rough patch. We were separated and found our way back to each other. We'll keep the ugly parts cute and protect the guilty where applicable."

"You two getting back together is so sweet," Garnet said wistfully. "I wish…"

"What?" Cindy asked.

"Nothing," Garnet shook her head.

"Maybe Garnet has something to hide," Jack frowned.

"I don't," Garnet sighed. "I really don't."

"You are my nephew's mother," Jack said. "I just found out last week."

Cindy raised an eyebrow. "Oh really, which one of his brothers is it?"

"Chex," Garnet groaned. "I wasn't hiding it; I just never told anyone in your family."

"Or yours," Jack said. "If Garwin knew, he would have said something."

"That's true," Garnet said. "But your brother was not the fatherly type; he made a big deal of not passing down his genes, and I wasn't going to upset him unnecessarily by telling him that the one thing he didn't want to happen did, so I kept silent and went on my merry way."

"I understand," Jack nodded. But, as Neon's family, it

would have been nice to know; we wouldn't have to tell Chex, though I don't see how we could keep it a secret. I hope you can share Neon with us now that Chex knows, and it's all in the open."

"Yes, of course," Garnet nodded. "I'd have no problem with that."

"Good, I'll do your documentary," Jack said. "Cambria and I have a story to tell."

"Thank you," Garnet smiled.

He walked away.

Garnet turned to Cindy. "That's a relief. I had really wanted his story."

Cindy laughed.

"Where's Nicky and Orandy?" Garnet asked.

"They went to the States for the summer," Cindy said. "They took their daughter to meet their family in Atlanta for the first time."

"Oh," Garnet nodded. "That's nice. I had really wanted to interview them. Do you and Derrick still co-parent Jason with them?"

"Not really," Cindy said. "Jason adjusted to having Orandy as his father. He does come over to our house regularly, but by and large, we leave Nicky and Orandy to work on their family without our interference. They are a tight unit, as it should be. We have our hands full at the moment; we had twins a year and a half ago, a boy and a girl, Celest and Cairo."

"Oh, that's precious," Garnet said.

"My friend Camille, remember her?"

"Oh yes," Garnet nodded. "Camille with the red hair and infectious laughter."

"That's right. She had a girl a year ago. We joke that our daughters will be the next generation girl friendship squad."

"In twenty years, this neighborhood will have another group of intriguing stories," Garnet mused. "Maybe Neon's story will be a part of it, along with the Wileys, the Nelsons, the Knights, the Silvers, and any other new family that may come in."

"Let's hope they have less drama," Cindy grinned.

"It's karaoke time!" the MC announced. "And we have our own local celebrity, Garnet Silver, in our midst. Maybe she wants to start us off with this section of the program; I have 'No Promises' lined up in the queue as our first song."

Garnet groaned. "That's why he was grinning at me like that when I came in."

"Oh my," Chevelle clapped her hands and looked at her. "I love that song. Are you going to sing for me?"

"Yes," Garnet said. "Of course, anything for the birthday girl."

She ended up doing all the songs. That's what you get for crashing a party.

****

Fortunately, she only had to call Aunt Bunny to secure her interviews with the Nelson family.

"Of course, we'll appear in your documentary," Bunny said after enquiring about her health and chitchatting about life. "You couldn't do a documentary without us. We are the most interesting family in Crimson Hills!

"Well, other than yours, of course, and maybe Maud Beecher. Did you hear about Charles?"

"I did," Garnet grinned. She could always trust Aunt Bunny to accommodate her.

"Thank you, Aunt Bunny," she said huskily. "And I mean, thank you for everything."

Bunny answered just as huskily. "Anything for the Silver children. I love each of you as if you were my own. We should throw a party; so much has happened lately. We need to celebrate."

"True," Garnet said. "Patti was thinking of a massive party after Leonard Crooks' sentencing hearing."

"Excellent idea," Bunny said. "Tell her to call me."

****

Wednesday started with rain and a drowsy Neon who climbed into her bed in the early hours.

Both of them overslept because of the calming sounds of the rain. She ran around getting him ready for school.

When Garwin came to get Neon, she kissed him on the forehead and said, "No swimming for you today."

"Why?" Neon asked.

"Because it's raining," Garnet said.

"It's a pool," Joy said in the background, sitting at the breakfast nook and drinking her coffee. "What's the worst that could happen? The water is wet, just like the rain."

Garnet shook her head. "He could catch a cold."

"Viruses cause colds, not rainwater," Joy snorted. "I can't believe you are Gen Z and don't know this. Don't you people always scoff at our old wives' tales?"

"Okay, I stand corrected. Let me go and get his swim things," Garnet took off down the hallway and rummaged through Neon's things. She saw him off and proceeded to get ready.

She took a look in the hall mirror and inhaled deeply. Mr. Hudson would probably not recognize her. She was in a tailored dress, her hair in waves down to her mid-back, and she had applied light makeup. She was going for a professional look.

"Your teacher will give you an A without you doing the project," Joy chuckled behind her. "Is he male?"

"Yes," Garnet nodded. "I wasn't trying to impress my teacher, though. I'm trying to exude an air of professionalism. When I was at the school before, I had a tomboy reputation that I carefully cultivated because I didn't want to deal with being judged for my looks."

"You are pretty and wise," Joy kissed her on the cheek. "You are beautiful inside and out. Go and make waves, my love."

Chapter Fifteen

The instant she stepped into Mr. Hudson's office, she felt as if she truly was making waves. He looked at her with his mouth half open, forgetting to close it. And then he caught himself.

"Garnet Silver, my goodness," Mr. Hudson stood up, shook her hand, and then told her, "Have a seat, have a seat."

Garnet sat down.

"I am so happy you're finishing the program," he said. "You know, somehow, I didn't expect you to. A girl like you with such beauty, I expected to be off the market by now."

He looked at her ring finger and then back to her face, "I expected you to be married to one of those rich men who want a trophy wife."

Garnet frowned. "Mr. Hudson, I don't know if I should be insulted or feel complimented."

"Call me Jeffrey," he said. "It's an awkward compliment. So, how have you been, Garnet? I expected more music from you since that duet with DJ Duke."

"It didn't quite work out that way," Garnet said. "I went on the cruise ship route after I had my son."

"Oh yes, yes," Mr. Hudson looked at her curiously. "You had a son. That was the reason you skipped the final project."

Garnet nodded.

He seemed to be waiting for more information, but she kept her expression neutral and returned the topic to the issue at hand.

"I am so grateful that the school has allowed me to finish. So that I can draw a line under it."

"Oh yes, we do that for our students, and you were exceptional." He cleared his throat. "Well, do you have the outline?"

"Yes," Garnet said. "Three pages double-spaced." She handed it to him.

Mr. Hudson looked it over. "Interesting, I expected you to do a musician like everybody else, but you're doing several stories on the community of Crimson Hills. I like this.

"I'm looking forward to hearing more about these people. Garnet, you have always been original."

Garnet nodded. "Well, I hope to make the deadline. See you in eight weeks, Mr. Hudson."

"Jeffrey," he said. "Technically, you are not my student. I am just your project supervisor. I won't be grading your project. I am supposed to check on you weekly to find out how you are progressing."

"Okay, Jeffrey." She got up. "I will speak to you soon."

"I'm actually heading out myself," he said. "I'll walk you to your car."

"Are you seeing anyone?" He asked when they were on their way to the parking lot.

Garnet was stumped. Was he really checking for her now?

She didn't want to tell him no and then have him suggest they date. She struggled to wiggle out of the conversation when she saw Chex leaning on her car.

Chex!

She must have gasped. Mr. Hudson looked at her and then in Chex's direction.

Mr. Hudson cleared his throat. "Oh, I'm sorry, I didn't know you two were still a thing."

Garnet didn't know what she mumbled. She knew that Mr. Hudson went over to Chex, they shook hands, said something to each other, and then he turned to her.

"I'll be keeping in touch, Garnet. Are Fridays convenient?"

"Yes," Garnet nodded.

He walked away, and Garnet turned to Chex. "Hey."

"Hey," Chex grinned, that deep dimple appearing at his mouth. "You look like you saw a ghost."

"I, uh, I never expected to see you again," Garnet said.

Chex nodded. "But here I am."

"How did you know I was here?" Garnet asked.

"I went to Silver Manor. Your aunt said you were handing in your project outline."

"You spoke to Aunt Joy?"

Chex nodded. "And your father, too."

"Oh," Garnet said, curiosity in her gaze.

"They're cool people," Chex said. "I wonder why you didn't let me meet them before."

"We didn't want to involve our families, remember?" Garnet said. "I never met your brother Phillip. Of course, I knew Jack; he is one of my brother's closest friends."

Chex raked his eyes over her and then looked back into her eyes. "You look gorgeous, as usual."

"Thank you," Garnet nodded.

"No wonder Hudson had his tongue out, almost salivating

while talking to you."

"He didn't have his tongue out," Garnet said.

"That man still has the hots for you, doesn't he?" Chex said. "You can't blame him. I understand it."

"If you'll excuse me," Garnet cleared her throat. "I'm going home. I have eight weeks to do a documentary."

"I have a proposal," Chex said.

"I'm listening." Garnet crossed her arms and stared at him.

"I need someone to work with me on a mental health documentary."

"When?" Garnet asked.

"For the summer," Chex said.

"I have my own documentary," Garnet said, shaking her head. "I need to do it to get my degree."

"What's it about?" Chex asked.

"I decided to do it on the people of Crimson Hills. They are all interesting. I will have to do some gymnastics to fit all their stories in thirty minutes. I am starting with Winter Wesson and then working down the list," Garnet said. "I just handed in the outline to Mr. Hudson."

"I'll help you," Chex said. "I know all about Winter Wesson."

"You do?" Garnet laughed.

"I do," Chex nodded. "A long time ago, Maud and I had a book club. We used to read his diaries, and I wrote a couple of songs based on his adventures; you can use the music."

"Wow!" Garnet widened her eyes. "Thanks."

"I wrote the song beats when I was locked up in the dark, I used the words from his poems," Chex smiled. "Come to think of it, Winter Wesson was an inspiration."

"Can I put that in my documentary?" Garnet asked. "The impact of Winter Wesson nearly three hundred years later."

"On one condition," Chex said, "help me with my

documentary."

"But I am staying in Crimson Hills for the summer," Garnet said. "I want to do some interviews with people all over the community. My son is going to school here for the summer, and he is loving it. I have no intention of uprooting him. You live in Kingston; it's not going to work."

"Apparently, I'm staying in Crimson Hills for the summer, too," Chex said. "What a coincidence."

"Where?" Garnet widened her eyes.

"Knightsbridge," Chex said. "Jack has guest cottages near the waterfall. It would be a great opportunity to sort out some mental health issues, get to know Neon, and work with you."

Garnet stared at him wordlessly, then shook herself out of the inertia his statement had caused. "You want to get to know Neon?"

"And get back in your good graces," Chex said. "So, what's your answer?"

"It's going to be too much work to do your documentary and mine," Garnet muttered.

"When has that ever stopped you?" Chex asked. "You have gotten soft."

"I haven't," Garnet sighed. "Okay, I'll work on your documentary with you."

"Good," Chex said. "We have a meeting with Dr. Charles Payne in an hour."

"That's a crazy coincidence," Garnet said, "because I have him down as one of the people I need to interview for my project."

"Why?" Chex asked.

"He is Maud Beecher's son, and a direct descendant of Winter Wesson."

Chex laughed.

"What's so funny?" Garnet asked.

"I didn't know my first day here would have been so intriguing," Chex said. "You have to tell me more over lunch after we meet with Charles."

****

Charles was one handsome fellow. Garnet thought when she saw him. He shook their hands and launched into how grateful he was that they could help.

"I quickly realized I was in over my head," Charles said. "My wife and I thought we could do this together, but we don't have the skills to turn this into a quality production. And then Dr. Henry called and told me about you, Chex. He said he wanted you in Crimson Hills as part of your therapy and that your company is one of the best in the business."

"Yes, he's right," Chex nodded. "I was diagnosed with CPTSD, and my company is one of the best in the business."

"What's that?" Garnet looked at Chex, alarmed.

"Complex Post-Traumatic Stress Disorder," Charles answered. "That means Chex was diagnosed with a condition resulting from prolonged exposure to traumatic events, which has had a profound impact on his mental and emotional well-being."

"Oh," Garnet exhaled, realizing she had been holding her breath. "That actually explains a lot about him. I mean, a lot."

Chex shook his head. "Let's talk about the project at hand."

"Yes," Charles said. "We have fifteen stories. If we do five stories each and make it a three-part series, each part could be two hours long."

"So that's five stories stuffed into two hours?" Garnet murmured. "That's twenty-four minutes each."

"Is that doable?" Charles asked.

"Depends on the footage," Garnet said.

"We have a lot of footage. Lots of interviews from family and friends, of each person," Charles explained.

Chex whistled. "Okay."

"I know it's going to be a lot of work," Charles said, "but we are willing to pay for it. And, of course, I am here to collaborate with you each step of the way."

"We'll need you for guidance," Chex said. "I'll do one story and get your feedback if that's the direction you want to take."

Charles nodded. "Where will you be staying?"

"At Knightsbridge," Chex sighed.

"Good," Charles nodded. "I'll stop by on my way from work."

"Give us at least one week to put together one story," Chex said, "and then you can give us feedback."

Charles nodded. "Call me, I'll come running. I am so relieved that you are going to do this." He handed Chex a thumb drive with his files.

"Did Aunt Bunny or Maud say anything to you about my documentary?" Garnet asked.

"Oh yes, Garnet," Charles nodded. "Both my mother and mother-in-law commanded me to work with you, and Mercedes said she would coordinate with you on time."

"Oh good," Garnet nodded. "I'll call her."

****

They agreed on having lunch at Silver Spoon restaurant because oxtail was on the menu.

"I have been looking forward to this all day," Garnet said when Marie brought their food.

"Oh, it's you, the heavy tipper," Marie grinned broadly. "You are welcome here anytime, day or night, Mister."

"My name is Chex," Chex said and smiled.

"And if Garnet is giving you a hard time, I'll talk some sense into her," Marie said fervently.

"I'll bear that in mind," Chex nodded. "Thank you, Marie."

Garnet chuckled when Marie left them. "She will tell everyone in the kitchen that you are back. The last time you were here, you were very generous with your tip."

"It was all a blur," Chex said wryly. "One second, I was heading to my father's funeral; the next second, I was having a panic attack, and then I saw you and Neon. And I realized what I had missed out on. My life hasn't been the same since."

"So you are not just back because of the documentary?" Garnet asked.

"No," Chex said, "I am back because I saw you again and discovered you had a son. My son. I still can't believe it."

"Sorry," Garnet said, "but when I found out I was pregnant, there wasn't a thought of not going through with the pregnancy."

"I know, I am glad you went through with it," Chex looked at her, his light brown eyes compelling.

Garnet looked down at her plate and decided to start eating even though nervous flutters were in her stomach.

"So you'll come by later?" Chex asked. "At the very least, we need to talk."

"I'm not sure," Garnet said. "I don't want to disrupt Neon's nightly routine."

"What's his routine in general?"

"Well, on the weekdays, I drop him at school at nine and pick him up at three. He swims in the pool at the townhouse or goes to football practice with Garwin between four and six. On the weekends, we've been going to the beach and outdoor picnics; he loves those."

"So what if you take him with you to Knightsbridge? And do all of those things there? Instead of going to the beach, you can go to the waterfalls, and there is a vast farm where you can have many picnics. Danger can drop him to school in the mornings and pick him up. He can be Neon's personal chauffeur for the summer. He is staying at one of the workers' cottages and won't have much to do. This summer will be a long holiday for him."

"You want me to move to Knightsbridge?" Garnet asked. "With you?"

"Yes," Chex said, "and take Neon with you."

"Is this a roundabout way of saying you want to get to know him?" Garnet asked. "Or is this a way for the two of us to reconnect? What's the game plan?"

"Yes to all of the above," Chex said. "So what's your response?"

"I don't know," Garnet said. "I'll think about it, weigh the pros and cons, and get back to you later."

Chex nodded, but he looked frustrated. She wasn't going to fall back under his spell after so many years. He must be dreaming if he thought she was that gullible.

But maybe she was, she thought while driving home. She felt differently around Chex, a feeling that could not be replicated around anyone else. It was missing from all of her interactions with the opposite sex in the five years since they had been apart.

She hadn't felt so alive in years, and she was seriously thinking of taking him up on his offer to stay at Knightsbridge so that he could get to know his son and they could work on their relationship.

But first, she was going to read up on what Complex Post Traumatic Stress Disorder was and see what she was up against.

Chapter Sixteen

Chex drove up to Knightsbridge. He felt twinges of the panic attack from the last time, but it wasn't as severe as the day of the funeral. He breathed in and out through it. He stopped at the security post at the front, where the security guard looked familiar.

"Chex?" He widened his eyes.

"I am sorry," Chex said, "I recognize the face, but…"

"It's Orville Lewis!" the security guy grinned. "My father was one of your father's followers. I was much younger than you when you ran away. You were our hero. You set a template for the rest of us."

Chex grinned. "Really?"

"Yes, really," Orville nodded. "Luckily, the cult disbanded after that, and my father worked on the farm. I eventually left, and ironically, the security company I work with assigned me to Knightsbridge. So I am basically back home."

"Ah," Chex nodded. "I never thought I would come back

here, ever."

"Things are much different now," Orville said. "You won't recognize the place. By the way, Jack will be waiting for you at the new cottage. It's to the left of the fork in the road; there is a sign."

"Thanks, Orville," Chex saluted him and drove to the fork in the road.

The place was nothing like what he remembered; even the landscaping was unrecognizable. Four roads led to various places. One arrow pointed to private residences - Knightsbridge Drive. Another arrow pointed to fisheries and dairy farms. One arrow pointed to the admin and greenhouses. The last one pointed to the village shop, seed store, and herb garden. Underneath that sign was another arrow that said to the waterfalls and guest villas.

He would take the one to the waterfall and villas, of course. Back in his day, there was no road; there had only been a dirt track. Phillip had not been joking when he said the place was not like what he remembered. The landscaping on the way to the villas was obviously new; the poi trees that bordered the roadway were still young. You could tell that Jack's vision was to have the roadside blanketed with poi blooms on both sides when you drove towards the cottages. It was going to be beautiful.

He noted the solar streetlights along the roadway and the fences keeping the cows on one side and sheep on the other. He slowed down to make sure it was sheep. It was a working farm, indeed.

"Go, Jack," he whispered under his breath. He had no doubt his brother was the one who made things look attractive. His father wouldn't have cared about these kinds of details.

He heard the faint roar of the waterfalls when he approached the villa. He turned off the AC and wound down his window. It was cool outside. And it was summer! He had forgotten that about the higher elevations of Crimson Hills. Summer nights could get downright nippy.

The villas were impressive, and he didn't impress easily. They were on an incline overlooking the countryside. The cobblestone driveway was flanked with tropical flowers, and the villa was part stone, part neutral shades, and with many windows.

Jack was waiting out front of the first villa.

"Welcome to Knightsbridge Farm," Jack grinned. "I must confess I had to come here and see you for myself; I didn't quite believe when you said you were coming by for the whole summer. You do realize that this is as rural as it gets, don't you?"

"Yup," Chex nodded. "How dark does it get at night?"

"It's not pitch black. We have solar lights," Jack grinned. "And Wi-Fi and running water. Let me show you around and help with your bags."

Jack opened the stylish wooden door into the living room, revealing a spacious area with tasteful furnishings; the distinct wood finish of the lignum vitae wood was evident everywhere. It was warm and inviting and looked identical to several luxurious spots he had been to in the past. He said as much to Jack, who beamed at him.

"I'll tell Cambria what you said, this was her project."

"How is she these days?" Chex asked.

"Great. Busy," Jack smiled. "She wants to know when we will have a family get-together; her family always has get-togethers and meetings. She thinks we should do the same."

"That's not a bad idea," Chex said as he walked toward the patio doors. Weak sunlight streamed through, casting a golden glow over the room. The air was filled with the scent of fresh flowers, mingling with the subtle aroma of cedarwood from the polished floors. I had forgotten how lovely this place was," Chex said, looking out at the greenery, the rolling hills, and the blue bands of sea in the distance.

"One-third of it is yours," Jack said. "Dad said in his will that all of this property, the business, everything should be left to his sons: Phillip, Chex, and Jack."

"How touching," Chex snorted. "The monster remembered me. I am surprised he remembered I exist."

"He remembered," Jack said grimly. "He couldn't speak properly in his last moments, but I could swear he said sorry with tears in his eyes. Then he said, 'Tell Chex, Phil… sorry.' I leaned forward and said, 'I forgive you, Dad,' and he squeezed my hand."

"Oh, really?" Chex raised an eyebrow and looked back at Jack. "How touching."

"I was touched," Jack said. "For some reason, I am not bitter about him anymore. Closure is a good drug. Am I happy he is not around anymore? Yes. Am I sad that he is gone? No. I feel indifferent. Even Mom seems indifferent."

"How is she?" Chex asked.

"Like a load has lifted off her shoulders," Jack shrugged. "I don't think she has been happy for several years. She just put her game face on and stuck it through with Dad. Cut her some slack when you see her, will you? She is coming here today hoping to talk."

"One conversation will not make up for her years of neglect," Chex sighed. "I came here to work, reconnect with Garnet, and get a feel for fatherhood."

"I couldn't believe it when I heard you were a father," Jack said. "Cambria and I went to one of the football matches to see Neon. I have always heard Garwin talk about his nephew; little did I know he was my nephew, too."

Chex nodded. "I made a royal mess of that; now I have to play catch up. Can you give me the grand tour so I can figure out which room I will turn into my editing room?"

"There is a library," Jack said, "with built-in bookshelves and its own patio. Okay, let's start the tour."

They moved through the living room and into the kitchen, which boasted modern appliances and sleek countertops. From there, they explored the bedrooms, each more luxurious than the last, with plush bedding and stunning views of the surrounding countryside. Jack pointed out the library, which could double as an office. He left the primary bedroom last.

"And here's your room," Jack said, opening the door to a spacious bedroom with a king-sized bed and en-suite bathroom.

"This is nice," Chex said, "you and Cambria did well. The word 'tranquil' comes to mind when I look at this place. The only problem is I am not a tranquil person; I love the hustle and bustle of a city. Up here is too quiet."

Jack laughed. "There is beauty in silence. Maybe you'll change your mind by summer's end and even sleep at night. Just in case, I left some melatonin gummies on the kitchen counter."

Chex snorted. "I don't sleep at night; melatonin gummies won't work."

"Try it," Jack said. "I'll call you tomorrow to check up on you. The housekeeper works from nine to four. She'll cook you breakfast and dinner; give her advanced notice if you want a special meal."

Chex nodded. "Thanks, man."

"I'll leave you to it," Jack said, "call me if you need anything."

****

After Jack left, Chex went about trying to make himself at home. He packed out his clothes in record time, eager to start working on Charles Payne's mental health documentary. At least this was something he could sink his teeth into while he waited for Garnet to make up her mind about staying with him.

He was rummaging through the well-stocked kitchen, looking for the fixings to make himself a sandwich, when he heard a vehicle come up the driveway. He looked through the front window and didn't recognize the car, but then his mother stepped out.

He groaned; he would have liked it if she had given him time to settle in. She knocked on the door twice.

Chex opened it. "Hello, mother."

She winced. Maybe his voice was too cold.

"Chex!" She made up for that by greeting enthusiastically. "How are you?"

"Fine," Chex stepped aside.

"Have you eaten already?" she asked, walking into the house with a stack of containers in front of her. "I have stewed chicken just as you like it and strawberry shortcake."

It was a peace offering; he would be petty if he didn't take it. Besides, he was hungry.

This was his mother, aging well; she was the feminine version of Jack with her narrow, youthful face, light brown skin with a smattering of freckles across her nose, and her impeccably turned-out hair swinging around as she walked.

How ironic, Phillip looked like their father, Jack looked like their mother, and he looked like neither of them. Even his outer genetic makeup had distanced itself from the

Knight family. He didn't know what to say to his mother; he never knew what to say. Deep inside, the vulnerable little boy in him had missed her. She hadn't been his abuser, but she was an accessory.

He cleared his throat. "I was just going to look about dinner."

Laurel smiled. "And now you don't have to."

She busied herself in the kitchen, opening containers and dishing out food. "I love these guest cottages. I think I should move into the one next door for the summer, and then we would be neighbors and get to know each other."

"Don't you have your own house?" Chex asked.

"I'm going to have the whole place renovated," Laurel said. "I spoke to Bobby Nelson about it at the funeral."

Chex nodded. "Okay."

"Do you want to see it before it is unrecognizable?" Laurel asked.

"No thanks," Chex said. "I'm only staying here because it is on a part of the farm I am unfamiliar with. I am not interested in stirring up any past memories. I don't have fond memories of this place."

"I wish I could change that," Laurel said as she carried over the food. "I have been so ashamed of my role in all of you boys' upbringing, especially yours. You went through more than Phillip and Jack. I gave my agency up to Maurice; I was a dutiful, submissive wife, and, in the process, I allowed him to discipline you how he saw fit."

"I didn't need to be disciplined," Chex said. "Most of the time, he punished me because he wanted to emphasize who had the power."

"You made it difficult by defying him," Laurel said. "You taunted him, Chex. It was always a battle of wills between the two of you. You wanted him to kill you. My pleas to you to just listen fell on deaf ears."

"I was a kid, your child," Chex sighed. "You should have been pleading with him to not be a maniac to all his children. Why did you stay with him for so long?"

Laurel thought about it and then cupped her chin. "You should eat. This is going to be one long explanation."

****

"I met Maurice when I was backpacking across Jamaica. I had just finished college with a degree in History and Archaeology, focusing mainly on Jamaica and the Caribbean. I felt frustrated after earning my degree, realizing I didn't know my country well. So I set out to explore. With no immediate need to find a job, given my father's wealth and my status as his only child, I had the freedom to do anything or nothing at all."

Chex nodded. He knew the story, but he patiently waited while she did the retelling.

"I visited the country's historical areas, highlighting the oldest building or town in each parish. I stayed at guesthouses, spoke to locals, and listened to their stories and legends. That's when I discovered there is more to this country than meets the eye.

"The first time I came here, I stayed at Crimson Rest. I bonded with the owner, Miss Lucy, who mentioned that her mother's name was Laurel, too. She also told me about the waterfalls and the intriguing story of Crimson Hill Great House. Initially, I only explored the great house, but when I returned, I visited the waterfalls."

"And there you met Maurice," Chex said.

"I did. I still can't describe the kind of pull we had toward each other," Laurel shook her head. "It's as if I knew that this was the place I should be; he was the man for me. My family was against the marriage. My dad pleaded with me not to go through with it, and I told him off."

"I guess everybody could sense that Maurice was not all there," Chex said.

"He wasn't like that at first," Laurel shook her head. "It gradually happened. He kept getting visions of an angel telling him to prepare for the end. I thought it was strange at first, but by the time I had Phillip, I went along with it. Eventually, I started believing when his angel friend told him about things that would happen, and they came through. I was a believer. I turned a blind eye to the other questionable things and just believed."

"I am quite ashamed to say I allowed a man who was mentally unwell to lead my life for forty-odd years," Laurel sighed. "I stopped drinking the Kool-Aid when Jack was born. Maurice kept urging me not to go into labor because Jack would be a citizen of the heavenly realms. And for the first time, I saw that he was unhinged. I was going to leave, but he begged me to stay. He said he would keep the children if I went. I didn't want to leave any of you behind with him. I reasoned that when you all were old enough, I would swallow my pride and have my father take you, and then I would map out my own exit strategy."

"You wanted to leave?" Chex asked.

"I did," Laurel nodded. "I went from being a free-spirited adventuress with a thirst for life to being trapped in the hills with a man who basically had me and my children as hostages. And every time I made to leave, he punished my children.

"He broke my spirit. I eventually stayed because I had nowhere else to go. I was trapped in a prison of my own making. Enough about me. Tell me about you and my grandson."

Chex chuckled. "News travels fast."

"Jack said he looks just like Maurice. I can't believe it," Laurel remarked.

Chex smiled. "You'll meet him soon. I invited his mother to bring him and spend the summer."

"I see," Laurel murmured, "well, that means one thing then."

"What?" Chex asked.

"I am definitely moving in next door. I want to get to know him," Laurel said with a sniff. "I can't make up for my years as a poor mother, but I am willing to try to be the best grandmother there is."

Chapter Seventeen

Long after his mother left, Chex sat on the patio, staring into the darkness, pondering what she said and concluding that she had been a victim too. Maybe he had judged her a bit harshly. But who could blame him? He had only seen things from his perspective. It was easy to think that he could have done better, but he didn't know what he would have done; he wasn't her. He knew she had been through a lot and empathized with her. His therapy was working.

Look at him being empathetic.

He glanced at the clock; it was seven o'clock. What would Garnet be doing now? He knew she couldn't leave Neon alone at home. So he would go there instead. He grabbed his car keys. It was as good a time as any to meet his son officially, to look into those eyes that were so much like his, and to pledge to be a better man than his father ever was. He was at Garnet's gate before he could talk himself out of acting so impulsively.

"I am at the gate," he said when she answered.

"Whose gate?" Garnet asked.

"Yours," Chex chuckled. "Let me in."

The gate slowly opened, and he drove through. "Which one of these houses is yours?" he asked. Then he saw her car and parked beside it. He had forgotten to ask her today how on earth her family was living like rock stars.

Garnet opened the door and grinned at him. She was in shorts and a T-shirt, her hair in a high ponytail and makeup free.

She looked so good; he stood back and appreciated her briefly.

He had been a fool to ever let this lady go.

"Welcome to my home," Garnet said, "Neon and I were just winding down before bed. Today was sculpting class, and let's just say he has a knack for it."

Chex smiled and walked through the stylish foyer and into the living room. The patio doors were opened, and a light breeze blew through. Neon was on the floor in the corner, happily putting together play dough. Garnet was obviously watching television; she had paused her program.

"Would you like something to eat or drink?" she asked.

"No thanks," Chex said, "I already had something."

" Is this visit just to satisfy your curiosity about Neon, or do you want to be in his life for the long haul?"

"The long haul," Chex said. "I told you I was serious about both of you."

"Well then," Garnet said, "I'll introduce you as his father. Know what you are doing, Chex, because I will not have my son going to therapy when he is older because of you."

Chex smiled at her fierce expression. "Trust me, I know what it is like to have daddy issues. My boy will not have that."

"Hey Neon, this is your father, Chex," Garnet called to Neon, who was concentrating so hard on his design that he hadn't looked up once when Chex walked in.

Neon looked up when Garnet called; he was midway through putting a red ball of dough on what looked like a green body.

"I have a Dad!" he exclaimed with boyish wonder. His eyes lit up with excitement. He looked at Chex and smiled. One of his front teeth was gone. "You are huge."

Chex laughed. "I suppose I do look huge from your perspective."

Chex felt a rush of emotions seeing him up close for the first time; he wanted to scoop him up in a tight hug, but he held back, not wanting to overwhelm him.

Instead, he crouched down to Neon's level, a warm smile spreading across his face.

"Hey there, buddy," Chex said softly, reaching out to tousle Neon's hair gently. "You're doing a great job with that playdough. What are you making?"

Neon beamed proudly, holding up his creation. "It's a robot! See, this is its head, and those are its arms."

"That's amazing, Neon!" Chex exclaimed, genuinely impressed by his son's creativity. "You're quite the little artist."

Garnet watched the interaction with a smile, sitting on the sofa and witnessing father and son meeting for the first time. It was a moment she had dreamed of for a long time, and now it was finally happening.

Neon's energy began to peter out after he excitedly told Chex about his day. Then he sleepily asked, "Am I going to see you tomorrow?"

"Of course," Chex nodded, "I'll be around hopefully for as long as I live."

Garnet blinked back tears. The promise Chex had just made meant the world to her.

"I hope you keep your promises, Chex," she whispered after tucking Neon in and closing the door.

Chex had stood and watched their nighttime ritual.

"When I make them, I keep them," Chex said as they moved into the living room.

He sat across from Garnet. "I am committed to being the best father I can be. I'd like to think I would make this decision after finding out you were pregnant. But I am not blaming you for keeping him away from me; five years ago, I wasn't doing so well."

"And you think you are doing better now?" Garnet asked.

"I am," Chex said. "I am not perfect, but I know what my triggers are and how to work on myself, which is more than I can say about the old Chex."

"I must confess I came home and researched what CPTSD was," Garnet whispered. "It's a lot, and it weirdly makes sense; you fit nearly all of the symptoms: difficulty trusting, avoidance of emotional intimacy, emotional instability, attachment issues, and communication challenges."

Chex sighed. "Yup, that was all me."

"And I thought long and hard about letting you into Neon's life," Garnet said, "because all of your symptoms can be negatives for a child too, not just in a relationship between a man and a woman. I mean, this is a lifetime job. You will never cease being a father, and frankly, I am not one of those people who think that a child needs his father. If a father is defective, he can do more harm than good."

Chex nodded. "I know. You are preaching to the choir. My father was the one who made me like this, remember?"

Garnet inhaled. "I am taking a chance with you on this, Chex. If you are not up to the challenge, say so now."

"I am up to it," Chex nodded, "if I wasn't, I wouldn't be here in Crimson Hills. This is the last place I thought I would be spending my summer. But then I saw you and Neon. And though I toyed with the idea of ignoring that I saw you again, I couldn't."

"So what's next?" Garnet asked.

"We work on the documentary," Chex said, "both of them."

Garnet nodded. "So, how is it going so far?"

"Great." Chex shrugged, "I spoke with my mom at length today; she told me how she fell in love with Crimson Hills and my dad and how she realized he was off his rockers, but she stayed for us. Every time she made to leave, he punished us, so she stayed."

"Wow." Garnet shook her head. "So, how was it seeing and talking to her again?"

"Surprisingly, anger-free," Chex said, "I asked her why she stayed, and she said she stayed for us. He told her she couldn't leave with us."

"So she's no longer the villain then?" Garnet raised her eyebrows.

"No," Chex chuckled. I wanted to tell her she should have arranged with Grandfather Eustace to come and get us, but I didn't. I assumed it was a complicated decision for her, and who am I to judge her decisions and life? She did the best she could."

"I am going through the same thing with my father," Garnet murmured, "he is so different from the man I thought I knew. Sometimes I pinch myself. Leonard Crooks not only stole this place from him, he stole my father's personality too because the man that came back from rehab is a totally different man."

"So Leonard Crooks was the one who fixed this place up?" Chex asked.

"Yes," Garnet nodded, "we are still reeling from the irony that he stole so much from us, but when it was restored, it was more than we had before."

"Karma," Chex chuckled. "Are you going to the sentencing?"

"I don't know. My dad and aunt want to go," Garnet sighed. "Are you going?"

"Only if Duke wants support," Chex said, "I assume Madge is being sentenced at the same time?"

"Yes," Garnet nodded, "how is Duke holding up? I remember how inseparable he and Madge were."

"At first, he was shocked; he was vowing to stand by her side, but in the last couple of months, he has gotten closer to someone else," Chex said, "I will loosely say he moved on, but who knows, it may be just sex.

"In my case, I never moved on from you. I tried to avoid the emotional attachment. I fought tooth and nail not to care about you, but you crept in and stayed," Chex looked at her intently. "I never stopped loving you. I may have had difficulty saying it then; I may have pushed you away because of it, but still, you remain."

Garnet gasped.

"It may have reached the point where sex with other women just didn't have the appeal," Chex shrugged, "and I told myself I was just getting tired of the whole scene, but I knew that it was because of you why I am not interested in other women anymore. If I didn't see you again, make no mistake, I would have come looking for you. I am positive I would have ended up here eventually. But I had to work on myself first."

"Chex," Garnet whispered.

"I want the whole package," Chex said, "you and Neon. If you'll have me, that is."

"Well, I..." Garnet felt as if her tongue was stuck to the roof of her mouth.

"Don't say anything," Chex said. "We'll revisit this after summer, and I'll need an answer about you staying with me over at Knightsbridge."

"Yes," Garnet whispered.

"Good," Chex nodded.

"Separate rooms, no sex," Garnet said, "we'll see where all of this leads by the end of summer."

Chex grinned. "Deal."

He shook her hand and smiled when he felt the tremor in hers.

"If I can recall," Chex said, "you were the one who couldn't keep her hands off me."

Garnet pulled her hand from his and tucked them together. "I will exercise self-control. I don't want to go through what I went through after our last weekend together when we parted for good. I sang 'Ti Amo,' the Laura Branigan version, at the top of my voice and cried at all my gigs for weeks after that."

Chex cleared his throat. "What?"

"I made a fool of myself for weeks," Garnet smirked. "I aggressively sang, 'How could you end it this way, After the love that we made? God, how I wish you had stayed. Can't you see that I just want you back?' And after a bout of crying, I would go back on stage and sing huskily, 'Where do broken hearts go? Can they find their way home?'

"I was a mess."

"Oh, Garnet," Chex cupped her face. "I am so sorry."

"My audience loved it," Garnet said, "but if anything, that time has taught me that I don't handle a broken heart well. And so, I am going into this with my eyes wide open. There will be no unnecessary entanglement for us. I don't want to be broken at the end of summer."

"You won't be," Chex kissed her on the forehead. "I didn't realize in all this that you were just as incredibly sad as I was."

"Of course I was," Garnet looked at him solemnly, "I loved you."

"I loved you too," Chex said, "but we wouldn't have made it. Not the way I was. This version of me is better, trust me."

Chapter Eighteen

"It's just until the summer is over," Garnet said to her aunt, who was looking at her packing up with her mouth half-opened.

"So you just saw him the other day, and now you are moving in with him?" Joy asked incredulously. "You act like the man didn't break up with you five years ago."

"We'll be in separate rooms; he wants to see Neon daily. And he wants us to make a go of our relationship again. It's a trial run. What's the worst that can happen?"

"I don't know. You may end up broken-hearted again, but this time, he will be in your life permanently because of Neon. I can't believe you are leaving your lovely townhouse to go live in the backwoods with this guy."

"Knightsbridge is not the backwoods. Have you ever been over there?"

"Not past the farm shop," Joy said. "And it is literally the back of the hills."

"That figures," Garnet said, "Chex said he is in a nice place, and if there is one thing about Chex, he stays in nothing less than luxury."

"Besides, it's different this time," Garnet said. "Chex is working on himself. I mean, he really is. When a man is working on himself, you have to respect and admire it. Some people will never admit they have a problem, much less work on it. We have a greater chance of staying together now. The absolute truth is, I never got over Chex. And I want this to work."

"Well, I liked him when he came here," Joy grunted. "He presents himself as smart and agreeable."

Garnet chuckled. "But?"

"There is no but. I hope he knows I am coming over to Knightsbridge Farm regularly to visit you and Neon."

"He won't have any problem with that," Garnet said. "Chex is not an ogre. He is, as you said, smart and agreeable. Just remember that this is not just about our relationship or Neon. We committed to working on a documentary and my school thing."

"Okay," Joy held up her hands. "I just don't want you to get hurt."

"And I love you for that," Garnet finished packing her suitcase. "So when are you leaving to go back to Kingston?"

"Tomorrow," Joy said, "but I will return for Leonard Crooks' sentencing. I am taking Sterling. We thought we should go. And Patti is arranging an after-party at your father's request. I want to be there for that, too."

"Okay," Garnet smiled. "Bring it on."

****

Chex wasn't joking when he said the place was nice.

Garnet drove up the hill and stopped in front of the first guest house. It was modern yet rustic and chic. Chex left the front door open.

She walked through and inhaled. "It smells like roses in here."

Chex was sitting at the dining room table. He smiled. "That's from my mother's greenhouse."

"And you are up at ten in the morning," Garnet looked at him. "How?"

"When I came in last night, I had that melatonin my little brother suggested I take, and wouldn't you know it, it worked. I woke up at eight, speed-watched hours of footage, spliced some pieces together, and ended up with an hour's worth of footage. We must boil that down to twenty-four minutes and then discuss the musical score. This one is about Orandy Wiley. He has schizophrenia, and his story is wild. We'll need a lot of dramatic music."

"Orandy?" Garnet nodded, "I was talking to Cindy about him the other day. I wanted him for my documentary, but he is gone with Nicky to Atlanta for the summer."

"He is amazing," Chex said, "I wish I knew him when I was living here. I can't remember seeing him. I am in awe of the things he has accomplished despite his illness. The man has held down a job, married a beautiful woman, and has two children. It hasn't always been easy; he admitted in one of the clips that when he didn't want children and then he found out Nicky had his son, he was afraid the boy would have schizophrenia because all his uncles had it.

"He said he still has days when he goes into his dark spaces and shuts down, but Nicky is always there for him."

"Let me see him," Garnet said. "I don't know him personally either. I heard he resembles Derrick and Lee."

"There is a clip here with him and all his brothers," Chex

brought it up on the screen.

"Oooh Lord," Garnet whistled, "they are eye candy separately but a whole candy store together."

Chex chuckled. "Put your tongue back in, stop your thirsting; most of these men are happily married. And you are spoken for."

Garnet grinned. "I am?"

"You are," Chex gave her one of his intense looks that made her shiver inside.

She dragged her eyes from his. "How do you do that?"

"Do what?" He asked innocently.

"Say so much with your eyes," Garnet sighed. "I will not give in, Chex, I am here to work and to allow you time with your son and nothing else."

"I respect that, and I will not breach your boundaries," Chex said. "I'll help you with your bags, and we can discuss song selections for Orandy Wiley's story."

Garnet nodded. "Good."

"One of Orandy's favorite songs is Michael Kiwanuka's - Love & Hate. We'll need the sync license for that as soon as possible."

"Love that song," Garnet said, "you can't break me down, you can't take me down."

Chex laughed. "I mentioned the song because of that line. You can make it your anthem for the summer. Dedicate it to me and my intense looks."

****

Their days fell into a routine. Garnet could scarcely believe how seamlessly they seemed to fit into each other's lives. Occasionally, she pinched herself that this was now her life. She worked with Chex from eight to two on the mental health documentary; Danger took Neon to school. They usually had lunch together, delivered from Silver Spoon Restaurant, and then Danger picked up Neon, and Chex hung out with his son for the rest of the day.

They had a mutual admiration going on. They both found each other fascinating.

Neon and Chex got on like they had always known each other. She usually left them together to go work on her documentary footage.

Chex had found a winning formula with Neon; they explored the seventy-acre farm together. When she saw her son in the night, he was tuckered out.

"What did you do today?" Garnet whispered after tucking Neon in. They were one week into living at Knightsbridge.

"Grandma took me to introduce me to her little friends," Neon replied.

Garnet looked at Chex, who was standing at the door. "What?"

"My mom moved in next door while you were away today," Chex said wryly. "She took him with her to introduce him around to everyone. They basically did a farm tour. From what I understand, he made some friends. There are some workers' children in his age group, and they had a blast. My mom said she has never seen a little person make friends so fast."

Garnet laughed. "I'm afraid he won't want to return to Kingston."

"When he came back, he declared this to be the best place on earth," Chex said.

"Oh my," Garnet snickered. "Neither of us are country-loving people."

"But there is something to say about the air up here: I am actually sleeping at night. I can't believe it," Chex said. "All

I had to do was eat two gummies before bed, and by ten, I am out like a light. I can't tell anyone this."

Garnet laughed as they sat on the patio. "Maybe it's not only the gummies. Maybe it's the fact that you are more contented and feeling less wound up than you have in years."

Chex glanced at her. "Maybe you have a point. But to be able to sleep at Knightsbridge of all places. The place that I hated the most."

"Do you hate it now?" Garnet asked. "Be honest with your answer."

"I am always honest," Chex murmured. "This part of Knightsbridge is perfect. Bathed in the golden rays of the setting sun, feeling the fresh breeze, looking over the greenery, I feel a sense of calmness I haven't felt in years."

What had changed?

Garnet waited patiently for him to answer if he hated Knightsbridge now.

"I don't hate Knightsbridge," Chex said. "I just realized this. I don't even hate my father and what he did to me. Right here, right now, I feel hate-free and balanced. I am fine."

Garnet smiled. "Good."

"But I have to test out this theory," Chex said. "Come on, let's go to the punishment house."

"Now?" Garnet widened her eyes. "It will be dark soon."

"It's the best time," Chex said. "I used to be left in the dark there. We need flashlights."

"Do you want to retraumatize yourself?" Garnet asked.

"Nope, you'll be there with me," Chex said. "I'll try to man up and not scream like a little girl. I'll ask Mom to stay with Neon while we are out. It will be her absolute pleasure."

Chapter Nineteen

They decided to walk to the punishment house. It was on the other side of the property, about two miles away. It was a nice evening for a walk.

"Tell me about your pregnancy," Chex said as they headed down the road. The road had seemed so tame when driving up but was actually steep.

Garnet panted a bit. She was slacking on her exercise routine; she needed to get back into it. Hot yoga had not prepared her for this kind of exertion.

"My pregnancy was relatively uneventful. I finished my final semester at school without anyone knowing I was pregnant. My penchant for baggy clothes meant I could hide it easily. I missed out on my final project, which I would do for the summer because I was too big to hide and needed to do a presentation.

"I went back to Kingston, was cuddled by my aunt. She kept badgering me about telling the father. 'When are you going to tell the father?'"

Chex winced. "I am sorry."

"There's no need to be sorry," Garnet said. "You were quite clear that you didn't want children. I had Neon; my aunt and brothers were there."

"You guys are close, huh?" Chex asked.

"We had to be," Garnet said. "My family history meant that the four of us needed to stick together. When Neon was six months old, I went back to work, this time in St. Ann. It was closer to Kingston, and I could go home on the weekends.

"I operated like that for two years, and then I sang one night at one of my regular venues, and this woman who is a cruise ship recruiter videotaped my performance. And invited me to join her staff.

"I was torn. I didn't want to leave my baby for too long. I would have to sign a six-month contract with only two weeks of shore leave out of that. My aunt encouraged me to do it; she had no problems caring for Neon alone. After all, she had taken care of me."

Chex slowed down, took her hand, and pulled her closer. "I can hear that you felt bad about it."

Garnet sighed. "I did it for the money. It was good money. I wanted to create a nest egg for me and Neon. And then six months turned into two years, and I came home a couple of months ago and decided, enough, I am not going back. I missed so many years, not a day more. And here we are."

Chex squeezed her hand. "Here we are. I am sorry you ever had to do that. Even though I said I didn't want children, it would have been my pleasure to support both of you financially. In fact, I am having my lawyer draw up papers to that effect."

Garnet reached up and kissed him on the cheek. "I don't

need your money, Chex."

"It doesn't matter if you do or not," he insisted, "you are the mother of my child; he is entitled to everything I have, and I have a lot."

Chex moved his head and kissed her fully on the lips. "Now I can't think," he whispered when they broke apart. "Why would you want to kiss a man who has been celibate for two years?"

Garnet giggled. "Maybe because I have been celibate for five?"

"Are you serious?" Chex asked, "You didn't break up with me and then sleep with a whole football team?"

"No," Garnet laughed, "I never wanted to. At first, I was a young mother, trying to keep my head above the fray, and then I was working. I was more interested in real relationships, not sleeping around. Only a few men are willing to do that these days. Then there's my son, and I had to think about who I wanted to introduce him to, and all of that, I…"

Chex pulled her closer and kissed her again. This time, he didn't let go easily. Their lips met with a longing that seemed to bridge the years of separation.

Garnet wrapped her arms around him, pulling him closer to ensure he wouldn't slip away again.

When they finally parted, their breaths mingled, and Chex looked into Garnet's eyes with a depth of emotion he hadn't felt in a long time. "I've missed you," he whispered, his voice raw with emotion.

Garnet smiled softly, her fingers tracing the contours of his face. "I've missed you too," she confessed, her voice barely above a whisper.

"Well, this is a new memory to create near the punishment house," Chex cleared his throat. "I recognize that tree."

"Let's kiss in front of the punishment house," Garnet said eagerly.

Chex laughed, and they walked toward the building. It seemed so small in the gathering dusk. And yet, when he was younger, it had been large in his mind. Standing in the clearing alone, an old cabin which had withstood years of neglect.

He opened the door, and it squeaked on its hinges. Inside was nothing; the old piano was gone. It was just an ordinary room with cracked concrete floors. The beams in the ceiling where his father used to hang him up to contemplate his sins were still there, looking strong like they could go for another hundred years. There was a cot in the corner.

The place smelled heavily of lavender. There was a basket of dried flowers in the corner.

"So, this is it?" Garnet whispered.

"Yes," Chex nodded. "It appears as if the farm hands still keep it clean."

He stood in the middle and looked around. "That's where I used to sit in the corner. That's where the broken piano was."

"That's where I found a loose board one day," he continued, "my father had left me in here for two days and forbade anybody from carrying me food or water. I think I got a little delirious. I walked around in circles, kicking every wood, and one shifted. I hunkered down in front of the small hole and howled like a dog. The guy who was supposed to watch me couldn't take it any longer. He gave me water and food through the opening, sat down, and talked to me. I was so grateful for that."

"Oh, Chex," Garnet wrapped her hand around his waist. "How old were you?"

"Fourteen or fifteen, more than likely fifteen," he

replied. "Phillip had escaped a year before. My father was especially bitter at that time about something I had done. I don't remember what. I probably dared him to kill me. He certainly tried."

"My generous guard fed me everything. I was famished," Chex continued. "He told his wife, and she sent food for me and all manner of delicious desserts. I gobbled them up like a starving boy, which I was."

"The next day, my guard told me my father was coming. So I set back the boards, lay on the cot, and pretended I was too weak to move. To tell you the truth, I was too full to move."

"My father was alarmed. He thought for sure after three days, I would be ready to eat anything. I refused the food and flopped around like I was really on the verge of death. He had to send for the car to take me home. When I got there, my mother was crying and screaming, 'You killed him, you killed Chex!' I think the whole farm could hear her.

"I remembered the pure look of fear on my father's face when he thought he had really killed me. I lay there and watched him as he panicked, and I felt a warm feeling of happiness.

"By the evening, I had gotten hungry and had given up the pretense that I was at death's door, but that look on his face when he thought he had killed me will always bring a smile to my face. My father had been afraid; weirdly, it gave me comfort."

Garnet chuckled. "That's twisted."

"No, it's not," Chex laughed. "It's a good memory. This is therapy. I am telling you a good memory while standing in the middle of punishment house."

"Let's go before it gets darker," Garnet whispered. "This place gives me the creeps. I can't imagine what it did to you as a child."

Chapter Twenty

Three weeks into June, there seemed to be a thunderstorm every other day. The afternoons would go from sunshiny and bright to dark and gloomy in the blink of an eye, and the lightning was especially vicious this year. On the mountain, you could see streaks of light everywhere.

"It's a good thing I have most of the footage I'll need," Garnet said, looking out and then squealing when the lightning flashed. "Because there is no way on God's green earth, I am going out in that. No way."

Chex and Neon found her skittishness funny. They were calmly playing Go Fish. She pulled the curtain over the patio windows and sat down beside them.

"We need to go next door for Sunday brunch," Chex said. "My mother has been fussing over it for a whole week."

"Who will be there again?" Garnet asked.

"It's just the family," Chex said. "Phillip and Pearl, Jack and Cambria, Pearl's daughter, Jewel and her husband,

Rory."

"I interviewed Jewel and Rory," Garnet said wistfully. "They are a solid couple. They got married so young, I love their love story. I can't believe Aunt Bunny didn't like Jewel at first. Aunt Bunny loves everybody."

"It seems as if you only got love stories," Chex said. "Are you subconsciously looking for a love story of your own?"

"What if I said I do?" Garnet smirked.

"You have it," Chex said, looking at her solemnly. "This is our love story. Every day I get up and see you, the day seems brighter. Every laugh, tear, and shared moment is our love story unfolding right here and now. It's been unfolding from five years ago; it just took some years and a man working on himself to get it going again."

Garnet's smirk softened into a gentle smile as she looked at Chex, her heart warming at his words. "You are going to make me cry," she whispered, reaching out to grasp his hand.

"Why are you crying, mommy?" Neon asked, concerned.

"I am not crying, baby," Garnet leaned in and kissed him on the forehead. "I said I felt like crying, but I was not going to. We are going to dinner at your grandmother's in a moment; I don't want to show up red-eyed."

****

The Sunday brunch was lighthearted and pleasant. Garnet was meeting Phillip for the first time, and she couldn't believe how similar he was to Neon. Laurel had shown her photos, of course, but seeing him face-to-face was staggering.

"When I just met Phillip, I accused him of not taking care of his children," Pearl told her fondly. "I thought he was the gardener. If I had seen Neon, there was nothing he could do to convince me he wasn't his."

Garnet chuckled. "It's genetics. Your story with Phillip sounds fascinating, too."

"Girl, didn't you say your documentary was thirty minutes?" Pearl asked. "How would you squeeze us in?"

"You two were instrumental in taking down Leonard Crooks. My family owes you that. Tell me how you did it again."

Pearl went into her story. "I ran Sensuous City for Leonard. I always knew in my mind that I was never free to go. He always said if you left him, you would be exiting this life permanently…"

They listened attentively.

"Now, I really want to interview you," Garnet said. "Are you guys leaving today?"

"No," Pearl said. "We are staying for a few days with Rory and Jewel. We wanted to go to the sentencing hearing tomorrow."

"So do my dad and aunt," Garnet said. My sister-in-law and Aunt Bunny are throwing a party at the end of August to celebrate. I need to add you to the invite list."

"We don't want to impose," Pearl said.

"You definitely will not impose," Garnet said. "It's a neighborhood celebration/end-of-summer party because we should get together and celebrate victories and blessings and all of that good stuff."

"Yes, mom," Jewel said. "I, for one, am happy that man is off the streets and will be no threat to you. I can't wait to celebrate."

"Okay, it's a date," Phillip looked at Pearl. "I don't mind coming back here now that Dad is gone. How are you finding it, Chex?"

"It is great," Chex smiled widely. Every day I am here is

just great, largely because I have Garnet and Neon with me, but I feel like a new man."

"I can see it," Phillip said. "There is a relaxed quality to you. I am loving it."

****

Leonard Crooks got life in prison without the possibility of parole. Madge got twenty years each as an accessory, that was sixty years in total for her.

Sterling told Garnet the news over the phone, and he sounded as if he was sobbing.

Joy came on the phone. "They are tears of joy. He can't believe he lived to see the day that man answered for some of his crimes."

Garnet looked across at Chex. They were doing their daily walk, where they discussed the music composition aspect of the documentary.

"Madge got sixty years."

"Yes, I know," Chex said. "Duke texted me. He didn't go; he sent someone instead."

"Is it bad that I hoped she would have gotten off with a less harsh sentence?"

"No," Chex said. "You knew her, it's natural. She made her choice to commit murder, not once but three times. The news actually shook me up and sent me straight to therapy. I kept getting flashbacks. I had a good, honest woman, and I let her slip through my fingers. What do I need to do to get her back and not be an ass next time around?"

"Oh really?" Garnet widened her eyes.

"Stop acting as if you don't know that you drive me crazy," Chex hugged her around the shoulders. "Crazy in a good way. You stir my emotions like no one can. I wanted to be better for you, but more importantly, I wanted to be better for me, too. So there you have it, Garnet, I am a work in progress."

Garnet stopped. "What song would you interject right here before we kiss?"

"Not A Perfect Man, Christopher Williams," Chex grinned. "I am not a perfect man, but I am glad you understand I want to be your heart and soul provider."

He started singing and twirling Garnet around. They danced in the road; a few farmhands passed them and smiled.

****

July on the farm was epic. Every fruit seemed to be in season, especially mangos. Knightsbridge had thirty different varieties. Neon was on cloud nine. Garnet feared that her little boy would burst from pure, unadulterated joy. When the six weeks of summer school were over, Laurel volunteered to keep him entertained while they worked. It was perfect; Neon went with her to the greenhouses and played with his friends. In the evenings, he went fruit picking with Chex and Jack. They had a whale of a time, climbing trees, swimming at the waterfalls, being a rough and tumble boy.

"You do know you've lost him," Cambria laughed at Garnet while she watched breathlessly as Neon, Jack, and Chex climbed a tree together. They were on a picnic by the waterfalls, the four of them and Neon. The rains had ended; it was a great opportunity to spend the day together. Garnet liked Cambria. It had been an instant mutual liking. And after interviewing her and Jack for the documentary, she liked her even more. When Cambria suggested a picnic, she jumped at the chance to hang out with them and get to know them better.

"I am beginning to realize that," Garnet said. "I am afraid Neon will be unhappy when we return to Kingston. He loves it here. He gets up in the morning with anticipation. He runs around in the day like a giddy puppy, then he retires at night, wiped out."

Cambria chuckled. "Life on a farm."

"With his father and uncle and doting grandmother," Garnet sighed. "He is happy."

"He has his aunt, too," Cambria said. "I am just a little busier these days because Jill had the baby. We recently hired new staff to pick up the slack so I will be more available on weekends, but I intend to get to know Neon properly before the end of summer."

Garnet smiled. "I love how this side of the family has accepted him so wholeheartedly."

"Jack gushes about Neon so much, I am beginning to think he wants us to ditch the plan and have one of our own before our planned date of next year."

"Maybe he is just enjoying being an uncle for now. Follow your plan, have some time with just the two of you," Garnet sighed. "I don't regret having Neon for a second, but I wish I had a plan."

"I think everything is going exactly as it should," Cambria smiled. "You and Chex found each other again, and you had Neon before his vasectomy. Otherwise, you wouldn't have the loveliest little boy who has brought you both joy. I hope everything works out for the three of you."

****

Garnet interviewed Laurel on Wednesday to get some historical background on Crimson Hills and the Wessons in particular. The lighting was perfect; the late afternoon sun cast a golden light over her as she spoke. Laurel was an incredible resource about the history of Jamaica, its ties with colonialism, and how English settlers contributed to the island's cultural landscape.

She also highlighted how unique it was that Winter Wesson did not have slaves at the height of the slave trade.

"The Wessons were super rich because of their gold mining empire." Laurel said, "By the time Winter Wesson was born, they were well-established in the gold trade and were super rich. Winter could afford to go on adventures around the world and explore his passions.

"When he landed in Crimson Hills, Lord Winter Wesson was the second son of a duke. He married Beatrix Wilson at twenty, who bore him two sons and died shortly after. He was a young widower when he came to Crimson Hills, and all the settlers' daughters wanted to marry him."

When they were done, Garnet grinned from ear to ear. "You are a great resource. If you had gone into teaching, I wouldn't have minded taking one of your classes."

"I am happy to help," Laurel smiled. "I did think about teaching once, but I love it too much in the greenhouse. Farming has taken over my blood."

Garnet nodded. "It seems as if it has infected Neon too."

Laurel laughed. "Oh, what a delicious irony it would be if he ended up running this place in the future. A Maurice look-alike without the other qualities."

"Anything can happen," Garnet chuckled. "I should ask Maud if this is where Neon ends up."

Laurel smiled. "Oh, before I forget, I was meaning to invite your family over for dinner."

"That would be great," Garnet said. "My aunt is in town for a few days. Sunday is usually my brother's downtime. They hired a new chef so that they can take the weekends off."

"I know," Laurel sighed. "I am feeling intimidated."

"Why?" Garnet asked.

"You have four chefs in your family—your brothers, sister-in-law, and aunt. I am a basic home cook."

Garnet laughed. "I am a regular eater of both your cooking and theirs, and all I can say is your food could win prizes. Your ingredients are fresh, and you cook with love. Besides, they are not judgmental. I think they would be happy for the break from the kitchen."

"Good," Laurel nodded. "I think it's time for the Silvers and the Knights to meet in a social setting."

Chapter Twenty-One

The joint Sunday dinner was a success, but the party was still ongoing. There were two games of dominoes going on, and there was a fair amount of drama surrounding each game. When Garnet decided to take a sleepy Neon to bed, he protested. Joy followed her and stood at the door while Garnet tucked him in.

"I like it up here," Joy said. "I had no idea it was so nice."

"Told you," Garnet grinned.

"I see Laurel and your father are getting on like a house on fire," Joy said. "Why do I see more than one Knight Silver union in the near future?"

Garnet laughed. "Stop it. You are not Maud; you can't see the future."

Joy sighed. She walked out onto the patio. "I love this place. I had quite forgotten how much. I have been toying with the idea of moving back home."

"Really?" Garnet asked.

"Yes," Joy nodded. "There is nothing for me in Kingston. You are not coming back to live with me, and Neon will be with you. I have more family here than there, and when my nephews start their families, I'll be around to help with them. Besides, I can work at the restaurant to keep myself busy; they can always use the help."

"Sounds like a plan," Garnet said. "When are you thinking of making the move?"

"Gradually," Joy said. "I'd like to travel too. Maybe I'll meet a nice gentleman who will make me rethink the whole institution of marriage."

"You never know," Garnet said. "Just don't marry a boy young enough to be your son like your mother did."

Joy laughed. "If he's marrying me for money, he wouldn't get any. I left an airtight will. You are all already on my legal documents. There is no room for error. I learned from my mother's situation."

Garnet kissed her aunt's cheek. "It's a good idea to move back. I have a feeling Chex and I will spend lots of time back here, too."

"So you two are talking long-term?" Joy asked, excitement lacing her voice.

"Not yet," Garnet cautioned. "I am getting ahead of myself. It's just that it's hard not to think of us as a team."

Joy smiled. "It's working out. I will shop for a wedding dress, just in case."

"I don't know," Garnet said. "Marriage is a big commitment. I don't think Chex will ever be ready for that."

"If he loves you, he won't think twice about it. He'll want to tie himself to you without being forced to or prompted. I know you love him, but don't settle. You deserve to be a wife and not just a girlfriend. Call me old-fashioned, but marriage shows the world that you are each other's chosen partners, bound by love and commitment. It's beautiful to share your life with someone in that way, to build a future grounded in mutual respect and devotion."

Garnet nodded. "I appreciate your perspective, Aunt Joy. It's just... I don't want to push Chex into something he's not ready for. Our relationship is still evolving, and I don't want to jeopardize what we have by rushing into marriage."

Joy nodded understandingly. "Of course, dear. It's important to let things unfold naturally. But don't underestimate the power of love. You will know it in your hearts when the time is right."

****

Garnet sighed. Why was the marriage conversation still in her mind three whole days later? She should be concentrating on her editing. She was writing the script for Patti to read for the documentary, yet here she was, scrolling through an article that had caught her eye: How To Get Him To Propose.

There was truly a first for everything. A few weeks ago, she would have passed the article by and smirked, but after the conversation with Aunt Joy, she was reading it with an eagle eye.

Getting him to propose depends on his desire to be with you. What makes a man finally propose is his strong attachment to you with an intention to spend a lifetime together.

Encouraging a marriage proposal involves nurturing your relationship, fostering open communication, and creating a supportive environment where love can thrive. By focusing on strengthening your bond, understanding your partner's perspective, and fostering a sense of mutual respect and admiration, you can create the perfect conditions for a heartfelt proposal to unfold naturally. Remember to be patient, enjoy the journey, and trust in the power of love to guide you towards a future filled with happiness and commitment.

So basically, a man will only propose if he wants to and not because you nagged him into it. Garnet chuckled.

Chex was sitting in front of her at the other end of the table, his headphones firmly on; he was probably in the zone. He looked across at her unexpectedly and winked.

Garnet winked back.

Chex took off his headphones. "What does that mean?"

"What are you talking about?" Garnet asked.

"You winked back," Chex said.

"I thought it was the polite thing to do," Garnet grinned.

Her phone rang; it was Maud's number. She hurriedly answered.

"He is here," Maud said.

"Who is here?" Garnet asked distractedly.

"Winter Wesson," Maud said. "I explained to him what you wanted to do, and he said he was happy to help."

"I er…" Garnet was incredulous and excited at the same time. "Can I come up there now?"

"Yes," Maud chuckled. He is being quizzed by Miss Eve, the property manager. We told her that Winter Wesson was the one who ran up our expenses last year. Did she believe us? No. So now she knows, and she can take her questions to him."

Garnet hung up the phone and stared at Chex. "Winter Wesson is here."

"He is?" Chex frowned.

"I am going to do the interview. I am going to get footage for my documentary."

Chex chuckled. "I am coming with you. This is the interview I want to hear. I wonder how accurately he can portray the real man?"

"I have no idea, but we'll soon find out."

Chapter Twenty-Two

When she stepped onto Crimson Hill Great House grounds and met with Winter Wesson, she understood why Maud and her dad thought he was the real man. He didn't make matters any easier either. Maud introduced them to him in the living room of the Great House, standing under a portrait that looked just like himself.

Present-day Winter and the Winter in the picture were even in the same clothes. They had the same tousled black hair and vivid green eyes, and his skin was heavily tanned, almost nut brown. His eyes were remarkable against his skin.

"What in the world," Chex whispered beside her. "It's him."

"It can't be him," Garnet said.

"Mister Wesson," Maud said in her most deferential voice, "this is the young lady I was telling you about. She wants to do a documentary about the area."

"A documentary? That's a moving film," he nodded briskly. "Very well, I hear I'll have to sit still while you point one of your instruments at me?"

He turned to Garnet.

Garnet nodded. "Er… yes. Forgive me, but you sound like someone from one of those British films my grand-uncle used to watch, and you look like the picture behind you."

Winter laughed. "I expect I do look like the picture, don't I? It feels like I was posing for it just yesterday. Maud tells me I should not tell anyone I am the man in the picture. I am to say that I am a descendant of Winter Wesson, and I should speak of myself, I mean him, in the third person, for the purposes of not spooking you."

Garnet nodded. "Well, yes."

"Well, let's get on with it, then," he said briskly. "I have loads of things to do while I am here in this century. What were your names again?"

"Garnet Silver and Chex Hastings," Garnet responded, Chex seemed a bit shell-shocked.

Winter shook both their hands and paused before Chex. "Are you mute then?"

"No," Chex shook himself. "I was just taken aback by all the little details you got right about Winter. You have the same scar that cut your right eyebrow in two on your left brow."

"Oh, this was caused by a scuffle with a pirate off the West African Coast," Winter said. "The man's name is Murdock. He has a vendetta against me. He has tried to kill me three times so far."

Chex smiled. "So you read the diaries?"

"I wrote the diaries," Winter said, "but I am not supposed to tell you that. It defies your accepted reality, and I am not to upset you; it could tear the very fabric of space and time.

According to Maud's theory, the less you know, the better."

Chex chuckled. "You are good. But I bet you can't finish this poem: 'In the dark, I found my light, A glow that banished deepest night.'"

"With whispered words, I took flight, Embracing hope, dispelling fright. Through trials fierce, I dared to fight, In the dark, I found my light. With steadfast heart, I faced the storm; each challenge met a graceful form. Though shadows loomed, I stood reformed, A glow that banished deepest night. In every trial, a lesson learned, In every tear, a bridge returned. With every step, my spirit yearned, For in the dark, I found my light."

Winter finished the poem with a flourish. "I was in the bottom of a ship hiding from the locals at the time."

"You really read the diaries," Chex shook his head. "I added some lines to that poem and gave it to an artist of mine to sing. Have you ever heard of DJ Duke?"

Winter looked at him strangely. "I know many dukes. My father is a royal duke in King George's palace."

Chex nodded. "Of course. You are still in character."

"Can we do the interview in the library?" Garnet asked. "The light in there is perfect at this time of day."

"Oh, yes," Winter nodded. "My favorite part of the house. I have always had a scholarly bent."

He led the way, and Chex and Garnet followed him. While Garnet set up her equipment, Winter busied himself with the books.

"What are you looking for?" Chex asked.

"I need to find some history on Murdock Bartholomew, precisely where he is in 1720 and where he is going to be. I know the people of this century have everything recorded. Our lives are like stories to you, our homes are museums, our customs are strange."

"I guess you could say that," Chex nodded.

"Three hundred years after this, you will be stories, your homes will be museums, and your customs strange," Winter said.

"I guess," Chex shrugged. "I don't think about it much. I guess I would be shocked to go forward three hundred years and see what my descendants are up to."

"Maybe you can try it with the sundial," Winter mused.

"Tell me about the sundial," Chex said. "How does it work?"

"The man I bought it from in Jerusalem called it Hezekiah's sundial, which is rumored to make time stand still. I bought it from him because I thought it was a lark. I put it on my ship and made my way to the colonies. Sorry," Winter sighed, "you no longer call yourselves the colonies."

"I haven't heard anyone refer to us as colonies outside of a historical documentary," Garnet chuckled. "If you keep this up, with your accent and costume, people watching the documentary are going to think you are the real deal."

"I am the real deal," Winter said. "When I came to Jamaica, I put the sundial on my front lawn and admired its pristine beauty. My brother and I discovered, quite by accident, that the middle of the device could move. If you lined it up just right, at the proper time of year, it could push you to different points in time. So far, we have discovered that it goes exactly three hundred years in the future. We still don't understand it."

"Your brother would be Walker Wesson; he traveled with you everywhere," Chex said. "Your other brother, Wesley Wesson, was lost at sea for a while."

"He wasn't lost, he was captured by the pirate Murdock Bartholomew." Winter widened his eyes. "Where did you read this?"

"In your diaries." Chex suppressed a smile. This guy was a brilliant actor.

And then Garnet took over. They sat across from each other.

"Tell me Winter Wesson's story," Garnet began. "How he came to Crimson Hills. What made him live here, that sort of thing. You don't have to hold back any information; that's what editing is for."

****

"He was so good," Chex said as they drove back to Knightsbridge. "After a while, I began believing him to be the real Winter Wesson. I understand why Maud, Willie, and your dad firmly believe it."

"I do, too," Garnet covered her face. "Don't laugh. I know time travel is impossible, but how do you explain how he knows anything he just told me? He said when he came off the ship and walked inland, a hill seemed to be glowing crimson in the late evening sun. He told his crewmates he wanted to live on the hill with the crimson glow. He would happily spend his days sequestered in her beauty and living out his days in tranquility. The man's a poet in an old-school, corny kind of way. And he's so handsome."

Chex glanced at her. "You do realize that if he is seventeenth-century Winter, he is old enough to be your great-grandfather several times over. And if he is not Winter Wesson but imagines himself to be, that's a mental health problem right there."

Garnet laughed. "You are jealous. I thought you didn't 'do' jealous?"

"I was lying to you and myself when I said that. I do jealousy just fine," Chex squeezed her hand. "But only with you so far. I wonder why that is?"

"Could it be that deep down you have feelings for me?" Garnet asked.

"I don't have to search too deep," Chex said. "I do love you deeply, my lovely Garnet."

Chapter Twenty-Three

Garnet fretted and squirmed over her project while putting in the finishing touches. The deadline was tomorrow, and she wasn't satisfied.

"It's too choppy," she said.

"It's fine," Chex reassured her. "You did good work."

"But is it creative enough? Does it follow the million and one guidelines on the paper?" Garnet asked.

"Come over here," Chex was lounging on the patio. "Come and lie beside me, take a deep breath, and relax. It's done. The skies are full of stars and waiting to be admired."

"Is it your professional opinion that it is good work?" Garnet asked.

"Professional," Chex said. "Your project is a guaranteed A. I would show it at that community party that Patti and Bunny are planning."

"Don't you think I gave some people more time to tell their stories? And others too little?"

"No," Chex said, "your project is well-balanced. Everyone had enough time to share their story, and your approach to the project was thoughtful and considerate. You've put in the effort, and it shows. Now, it's time to trust in your work and relax. You've done great."

"What do you think about the music selections?" Garnet asked.

"Superb."

"And my handling of the introductory sequences."

"Divine."

Garnet snuggled beside him. "That's one of the reasons why I love you, Chex. Then and now, you always manage to reassure me and ease my worries."

"And why else do you love me?" Chex asked.

"You make me laugh, you make me think, you make me happy, you fill all the empty spaces. In eight weeks, I can't believe you weren't always here. You are good with Neon. I mean, it's amazing, especially since you didn't want kids."

"Do you want more?" Chex asked.

"Is that a trick question?" Garnet snuggled into his arm. "Didn't you get a vasectomy? Neon will likely be an only child."

Chex smiled. "It can be reversed."

"Well then, I'd consider more," Garnet looked out at the star-filled sky. "You are right; this is a nice view."

"What are your plans after the summer?" Chex asked after a short silence.

"I don't know," Garnet said. "Neon needs to go back to school."

"I could use another production coordinator at Right Vibes."

"Was inviting me up here to work on the documentary just a long job interview?" Garnet asked.

"No," Chex kissed her on the forehead. "I want you near me, that's all. I wouldn't mind if we shared offices, lived in the same house, drove the same car to work. I am finding that I wouldn't mind if we are joined at the hips."

Garnet chuckled. "It wouldn't feel right for me to sleep with the boss."

"Even if he is your husband?" Chex asked.

Garnet stilled. "What?"

"I came to Crimson Hills to get you back. I had to prove to you and to myself that I am better. A work in progress but getting better. I want you and Neon in my life every day."

Garnet reached over and kissed him.

"What does that mean?" Chex asked.

"You didn't ask me a question," Garnet whispered.

"Wait a minute," Chex said. "I think I need one of these before I propose. I had my cousin send it over; she made it five years ago in anticipation of just this moment." He pulled out the ring box that Lara had couriered over two days before. "Garnet, will you marry me?"

"Oh my goodness," Garnet gasped when she saw the ring. "It's gorgeous. Of course, I'll marry you. This is my dream come true."

"Do you know which song I would play right here?" Chex asked.

"What?" Garnet asked.

"Michael Bolton, 'I Promise You,'" Chex said. "I will promise you, yes I promise to love you for all your life, Love you every day and night, I will always be there for you."

"I promise you too," Garnet said, and they sealed their promise with a kiss.

Dear Reader,

THANK YOU for reading No Promises! I never intended to give Chex his own book but after writing No Fairytale, Jack's story, and Knight and Day, Phillip's story, I said why not? I liked his character, what should I do with him? And so, No Promises was born.

Technically, this is the end of the Crimson Hill Series. I am going to miss these characters.

At the beginning of the series, I wanted to write in a time travel trope for all the stories, but I decided against it. I did, however, keep some elements of it alive throughout the series.

If you stuck with the series this far you would have seen mentions of Winter Wesson scattered here and there throughout the story lines, and so I couldn't avoid it, I gave him his own story.

If like me, you like a good time travel romance, then you will find Winter's Eve, interesting. It answers all the questions about the sun dial and Winter's ability to time travel and what happens next with the Crimson Hill Great House.

Continue reading for an excerpt from this story, Winter's Eve. The book will be available on brenalbar.com. Before you go, please consider leaving a review.

If you have comments or suggestions, I welcome them. You can reach me and receive a reply at brenalbar@gmail.com.

Thanks again. All the best,

Brenda

Excerpt- Winter's Eve

It was the phone that woke her up. The incessant rings would not let up, and Eve felt as if she had just gotten into bed. The great house had just hosted a party. They had done thousands of them, but this time, it had been personal. Stuart Smithson, the head of the board of trustees, was celebrating his 50th birthday, and he had chosen this Wesson property to have the party.

Of course, as the property manager, she wanted everything to be perfect. Over the last few days, she had run the staff and herself ragged; a successful party would reflect greatly on her management skills, especially since she had slacked off for a couple of months while going through her divorce.

She needed this job now more than ever. Thankfully, Stuart and his guests had been impressed. She had stuck around until the last guest had left the property and the clean-up crew had finished restoring the place to its former glory. Then she had climbed into bed, practically dead on her feet.

When she slept over by the great house, she usually stayed in what was previously known as the counting house. The two-bedroom, one-bathroom cottage had been converted into a living area in the late 1800s. Back then, people would not count money in their house; it was considered bad luck. And so, they had a counting house separate from the main house. It was renovated and modernized with internal plumbing, but it kept the old charm.

She put the pillow over her ears and waited for the phone to stop ringing, but it started again. She searched for it blindly on the side table, knocking over her a water bottle and pushing her car keys onto the ground.

She answered without opening her eyes. She didn't know if they could be opened; they felt gritty and unrested.

"Good morning," she croaked.

Stuart's voice said. "It's afternoon. Can we meet for lunch? I've been hearing the most extraordinary things from Maud. I just saw a video of a dead ringer for Winter Wesson. I can't quite believe what I am seeing. Maud said you spoke to this fellow. I would love to hear everything you talked about and what transpired between you two. Who on earth is he?"

Eve groaned. Everything? Stuart didn't need to know that.

"Er, I'll be there in fifteen minutes," she said huskily.

She should have known Stuart would be up and gossiping with Maud. He and Maud loved conspiracies and intrigue where there was none.

He would have stayed at the back of the great house. The owner's suite was added in the early 1900s by one of the Wessons who occupied the place at the time. The new addition blended seamlessly with the rest of the house. They even used the same wild orange board for flooring and continued with the aesthetics from the colonial era.

She flung the pillow from over her head and looked around her suite. The décor was timeless and could fit in any era: dark hardwood floors, neutral white walls, and white linen drapes framed the tall windows. The four-poster bed made from mahogany dominated the room, and the antique side tables and writing desk were meticulously preserved.

The atmosphere of the place screamed opulence and history. She usually took a moment after waking up to pull the curtains and step out onto her patio to inhale the pure air of the countryside and admire the gardens immediately below. The blue and white African lilies were making a showy appearance at this time of year. Or she would look farther into the landscape where rolling hills converged to the sea.

Crimson Hill Great House had quite a view. She couldn't

admire much this morning, she didn't even pull the curtains, she stumbled to the ensuite bathroom. Thankfully it had modern amenities with a shower, a separate clawfoot tub, and hot and cold water. She would choose the cold water and stand in the shower, allowing the water to reinvigorate her. That was one advantage of having short hair, even though her mother had whined and complained about it. She had chopped her hair off after the divorce and wore it in a short, curly cap.

In her opinion, it made her look more sophisticated, and it was easy to care for but unfortunately, the shorter style took years off her face; though she was twenty-nine she looked like a teenager.

The Winter Wesson look-alike had called her a little girl when they had first met. Eve had tried so hard to forget the events from last summer, but apparently, she wouldn't have the luxury of doing so since Stuart wanted a blow-by-blow account about Winter Wesson.

"Who are you?" she remembered demanding of the stranger Maud had dragged into her office with a triumphant smile. The man was a carbon copy of the portrait of Winter Wesson in the ballroom: vivid green eyes, olive-toned skin, and black overlong hair.

His left eyebrow had the same gap as the portrait, as if it were parted by a thin scar. He was wearing the same clothing as in the picture, minus the jacket. He wore a loose, comfortable-fit shirt with ruffled cuffs and a high collar, a green silk waistcoat, knee-length breeches, stockings, and leather shoes with low heels.

She would have laughed if she weren't so shocked; he looked authentic. The only thing missing was the tricorn hat, like the one he had on in the portrait, and she had seen in the popular movie, Pirates of the Caribbean.

"He is Winter Wesson," Maud answered for the man.

He folded his hands and looked at her with his head cocked to the side, an air of irreverence to him, like he found her question funny.

"She is but a girl, Maud. Are you sure she is the one in charge?"

Maud had cackled. "She is in charge, and she accused me and Willie of running up her expenses when you came last year. Please let her know that you were the one who did it."

"I am the one who did it," he said, sitting in front of her desk and looking at her nonchalantly. "You are a pretty girl. Fabulous bone structure."

Eve had been shocked into silence, and then she opened her mouth. "I am not a girl. I am the property manager for this place."

"Pardon me," he chuckled.

"We have protocols for doing things; you are obviously a Wesson," Eve sputtered. "You should contact the board of trustees, let them know who you are, and proceed accordingly. It's inappropriate to bypass established procedures, regardless of your family name. You cannot just show up at the great house, sleep in our show rooms and make outlandish orders on my budget!"

He chuckled and leaned back in his chair. "I wonder which of my descendants was responsible for a board of trustees."

"You were," Maud said, "you wanted to preserve the history of the place for generations to come, and you wanted to ensure that your children's children would benefit from your legacy."

Eve groaned. "Maud, leave us. I want to have a word with this man privately."

"The name is Winter Wesson," he said, his British accent thick. "May I ask your name?"

"Eve Bloom, sorry, Blair." Eve cleared her throat. "I am recently divorced and still getting used to the name change."

"Interesting," he frowned. "I must read up more on divorce customs in these times. There is no divorce in my time."

Eve rolled her eyes. "Okay, enough. If you are going to stay here, please stay in the owner's suite. It's at the back of the building, and do not make any purchases with the great house money. Call the head of the board of trustees, Stuart Smithson, and he will happily work out an income for you. The trustees exist to serve the Wesson heirs."

"I won't be staying long enough for that, not this time around," Winter said. "The last time I was here, I was so excited I did go a little overboard. All of this is strange and yet exhilarating. The changes in this country, in the world, are mind-boggling."

Eve smiled. "Oh, they are?"

"If you went forward three hundred years, you would say the same thing, Eve Blair," Winter leaned forward, his eyes twinkling. "I find that the longer I look at you, the more exhilarated I feel."

"Get out of my office," Eve growled, "and please put the costumes back in the closet, they are delicate, we have to fight to preserve them."

He got up.

"And ask Maud to prepare the owner's suite for you. There should be no sleeping in the main house."

He laughed. "Another noteworthy change, the women are bossy in this century. I quite like it."

Discover Exclusive Offers and Be the First to Know!

If you haven't already, don't miss out on the opportunity to join my New Release Newsletter! Sign up today and become part of an exclusive community where you'll be among the first to hear about my latest book releases and take advantage of special prices.

Why join my mailing list?

Be the First: Get a head start and be the first to know when I release a new book.

Exclusive Discounts: Unlock special prices available only to subscribers. Enjoy limited time offers and save big on your favorite books.

Quick and Easy: Signing up takes less than 30 seconds.

To join, visit https://www.brenalbar.com/newsletter or scan the QR code below.

Thank you for your support, and happy reading!

The Crimson Hill Series

Where family drama, romance, and a touch of sci-fi blend seamlessly in the enchanting backdrop of a small town in Jamaica. Prepare to embark on an unforgettable journey as secrets unravel, passions ignite, and destinies intertwine.

No Goodbye (Book 1)
No Misunderstanding (Book 2)
No Ordinary Love (Book 3)
No Fairy Tale (Book 4)
No Letting Go (Book 5)
No Strings Attached (Book 6)
No More Mrs. Nice Girl (Book 7)
No Place Like You (Book 8)
Knight and Day (Book 8.5)
No Expectations (Book 9)
Ice and Fyre (Book 9.5)
No Surrender (Book 10)
No Time for Love (Book 11)
No Promises (Book 12)
Winter's Eve (Book 13)

The Wiley Brothers

Step into the world of the Wiley Brothers, where tragedy weaves an unbreakable bond and love becomes their guiding light. In this captivating series, follow the journey of six remarkable boys as they navigate the tumultuous path of growing up without parents, discovering love, and finding their place in a challenging world.

Between Brothers (Book 0)- How it all began…
For Pete's Sake (Book 1)- Preston's story.
Crossing Jordan (Book 2)-Jordan's story.
Fire and Walter (Book 3)- Walter's story.
The Perfect Guy (Book 4)-Guy's Story.
The Patience of a Saint (Book 5)- Saint's Story.
A Case of Love (Book 6)- Case's Story.

The Pryce Sisters

Follow the remarkable journey of the Pryce triplets as they navigate the complexities of growing up, discovering romance, and embracing the exhilarating challenges of the new adult years.

Baby For A Pryce- Book 1
Right Pryce Wrong Time – Book 2
Yours, For A Pryce- Book 3

The Jacksons

Prepare to be enthralled by the captivating saga of the Jackson family. In this gripping series, secrets unravel, paternity questions loom, and love blooms in the most unexpected corners.

Ace- Book 1
Deuce- Book 2
Trey- Book 3
Quade- Book 4

The Scarlett Series

Their patriarch died and unexpectedly left each of them a fortune. Watch as the Scarlett family navigate their way through the ups and downs of sudden wealth, family secrets, and the complicated dynamics of their relationships.

Scarlett Baby (Book 1)
Scarlett Sinner (Book 2)
Scarlett Secret (Book 3)
Scarlett Love (Book 4)
Scarlett Promise (Book 5)
Scarlett Bride (Book 6)
Scarlett Heart (Book 7)

Magnolia Sisters

They were the rejects. The worst of the lot, they grew up in a girl's home together and formed sisterly bonds. Each book in the series tells the story of a different girl and the unique struggles and triumphs she faces along the way. With themes of friendship, forgiveness, and the power of love, the "Magnolia Sisters" series is a heartwarming and inspiring read that you won't want to put down.

Dear Mystery Guy- Book 1
Bad Girl Blues- Book 2
Her Mistaken Dream- Book 3
Just Like Yesterday – Book 4

New Song Series

A group of friends started out as a church band, see how each of them navigate their personal and professional lives while staying true to their faith and facing challenges along the way. With themes of forgiveness, redemption, and second chances, the New Song Series is a captivating read for anyone who enjoys heartwarming stories of love and faith.

Going Solo- Book 1
Duet on Fire- Book 2
Tangled Chords- Book 3
Broken Harmony- Book 4
A Past Refrain- Book 5
Perfect Melody- Book 6

The Bancrofts

The Bancroft family delves into the inner workings of academia and the high-stakes world of university politics. The family wrestles with the pressures of maintaining their family's legacy, they must confront their own demons and navigate the complex relationships that bind them together. From unexpected love affairs and betrayals to scandals and secrets that threaten to tear them apart, this is a series that will keep you captivated until the very end.

Homely Girl- Book 0
Saving Face- Book 1
Tattered Tiara- Book 2
Private Dancer- Book 3
Goodbye Lonely- Book 4
Practice Run- Book 5
Sense of Rumor- Book 6
A Younger Man- Book 7
Just To See Her- Book 8

Three Rivers Series

Three Rivers Series, a captivating tale of love, redemption, and second chances set in a picturesque community in St. Ann's Bay, Jamaica.

Private Sins- Book 1
Loving Mr. Wright- Book 2
Unholy Matrimony- Book 3
If It Ain't Broke- Book 4

The Resetter Series

The Resetter Series takes a look at a rare kind of person, a person who can travel back in time, but they only have one chance to get things right if they go back! With themes of second chances, changing the past and the power of love, the resetters series is a captivating time travel romance that many readers have described as a page turner.

Never Too Late- Book 1
Never Say Never- Book 2
Now or Never- Book 3
Almost Never- Book 4

On the Rebound Series

Experience the gripping and emotionally charged On the Rebound series, where love, betrayal, and redemption collide in a whirlwind of passion and secrets.
Brace yourself for a journey filled with drama, cheating scandals, DNA questions, and ultimately, the power of second chances and finding love again.

On the Rebound- Book 1
On the Rebound Book 2

Standalone Books

Full Circle- After graduating from university, Diana wanted to return to Jamaica to find her siblings. What she didn't foresee was that she would meet Robert Cassidy and that both their pasts would be intertwined, and that disturbing questions would pop up about their parentage just when they were getting close.

After the End- Torn between two lovers. Colleen married her high school sweetheart, Isaiah, hoping that they would live happily ever after, but life intruded, and Isaiah disappeared at sea. She found work with the rich and handsome Enrique Lopez as a housekeeper and realized that she couldn't keep him at arm's length.

Love Triangle: Three Sides to the Story- George, the husband. Marie, the wife, and Karen-the mistress. They all get to tell their side of the story.

New Beginnings- Inner-city girl Geneva was offered an opportunity of a lifetime when she learned that her 'real' father was a wealthy man. Her decision to live up-town meant she had to leave Froggie, her 'ghetto don,' behind. She also found herself battling with her stepmother and battling her emotions for Justin, a suave up-towner.

The Preacher and the Prostitute- Prostitution and the clergy don't mix. Tell that to ex-prostitute Maribel, who finds herself in love with the Pastor at her church. Can an ex-prostitute and a pastor have a future together?

Historical Fiction

You won't want to miss out on these two captivating reads!

"The Pull of Freedom" tells the story of a slave family and their desperate struggle for freedom in Jamaica's colonial era. Follow the journey of these brave individuals as they fight for their right to be free, facing danger, heartbreak, and unimaginable obstacles along the way.

"The Empty Hammock" takes readers on a journey through time, as a modern woman finds herself transported back to the Taino era of Jamaica's history. Experience the wonder and mystery of this ancient culture through her eyes, as she learns about their traditions, beliefs, and way of life. With richly drawn characters and a beautifully realized setting, "The Empty Hammock" is a must-read for anyone who loves historical fiction that transports them to another time and place.

Short Story Collections

Di Taxi Ride and Other Stories- Funny stories about Jamaican life to make you laugh.